Finnigan's Point

Marc Antony Cutler

ISBN: 9798358896727

PublishNation
www.publishnation.co.uk

Preface

Finnigan's Point was written by our son Marc Antony Cutler and was published briefly on Kindle in 2012 with proceeds going to Great Ormond Street Hospital. It is no longer available on Kindle.

When we lost Marc to cancer in December 2018 at the age of 42, it became a labour of love, as his Mother, to get this book published in paperback, so his words were once more out there, so his friends and family and others could have a physical copy to keep and maybe buy a copy that could be shared to charity shops, hotel lobbies, airport departure lounges etc, across the world. It has been a long journey to get here and often a painful one re typing his words, but I am so happy to have achieved it for him.

He was working on another novel before he passed away and he wrote lots of poetry - sadly this is lost to us, but at least there will be one final printed book out there to keep his name alive for years to come.

All proceeds from this book will go to Children's Cancer UK, a charity very dear to Marc's heart.

Marc Antony Cutler was also the author of *The Choice Maker* published in 2016 and available in Paperback and Kindle on Amazon.

In Loving Memory of Marc 03.11.76 - 29.12.18

Forever in our broken hearts. Mum & Dad

MIZPAH
xxx

Chapter One

Terence Kane stood alone at his bedroom window watching the rain roll down like an endless stream of tears. It was only 5 am but as usual he was up and wide awake. His craggy weather worn face held the dancing shadows of the droplets in its age lines. The bags under Kane's eyes held the luggage of the sleep he'd been depriving himself of recently. Every sleepless phase felt like a longer cycle than the last. He couldn't explain it, there was no real reason. He could work hours upon hours, feeling as though his eyes would not stay open but when it came to the night his head would hit that pillow and his mind would re-awaken. It was as if his body had a vendetta against him, lulling him into a false sense of security only to make him endure the waking hours, watching the minutes tick by on the clock face, taunting him with the time remaining until the day would begin again.

He wasn't given to suffering stress, in fact in his own words he rarely gave a damn about anything, except of course himself. Forty six years old, a good looking rugged man, deep brown eyes like the finest chocolate with cropped dark hair, he certainly was a catch, yet despite this the perennial singleton. Many a time he had been compared to various Hollywood actors, but his own self serving personality had always resulted in the consumption of any flowering romance.

That's not to say he was selfish, he wasn't, but his life had always revolved around his work, there never really seemed to be time to concentrate on anything else. Now, past middle age and probably past his best, it seemed work would be all he ever would have the time for. A wasted life perhaps to some, but not to Terrence Kane. He'd only ever really been interested in making himself happy and in his own way, he was.

For the greater part of his life Kane had been a well respected Police Detective, but ultimately he outgrew the Force. Early on in his career the Police Force stood for everything he wanted to achieve in life, it always matched his own beliefs and goals. Eventually though it succumbed to Government bureaucracy, as most things seemed to, and both his and the goals of the Force went their separate ways, drifting like a melting iceberg.

Kane left the force and became a Private Eye, it seemed like natural progression to him. He served the public's needs as he'd always wanted to and continued to uncover the hidden truth around every street corner. In his mind Kane continued to be what he'd always aspired to be. In reality the well worn, slightly craggy man was a typical gum shoe for hire.

Maybe, had he concentrated just a fraction of the time spent making a wasted career, on forming some kind of meaningful relationship with the opposite sex, he would have found himself just as much the Private Eye, but at least married with perhaps a family. There's much to be said about building a career, but more to be said about gilding a family, something he would probably never know now.

All was not lost for him though, the years he'd spent honing his skills as one of the best Detectives around, were not a total waste, as they say form is temporary, class is permanent. Kane was now sought after property, even the Police themselves would occasionally use him. He was known for getting the job done, a perfectionist, never willing to settle for mediocrity.

Now he was still single, still alone, but a well worn and well used Private Eye, someone those who wished to keep their secrets safe and their internal turmoil locked away tight, turned to. In this town, that was regularly, the streets were covered in filth and not the kind the dustmen could remove on a weekly basis. The whole area was rife with scum. The levels of crime and the ferocity of the nature of the criminal acts had increased and increased year on year, but nothing seemed to be done about it.

Kane's town was not a nice place to live but despite it's faults it was an unrivalled place to work. Kane was never a wealthy man but now he was considerably better off than ever before. So much for the career and the Police pension, just about everybody out there had a secret they needed uncovered, which is exactly why he was ready to go out this damp, humid and miserable morning. There was money to be made and secrets and lies to uncover.

Standing there looking out of that rain soaked window into the blackness of the ending night, soon to be the dimness of the morning light, Kane thought about the previous day and the conversation he'd had with the man he was now working for, just a day later. Something had bothered him about Clarke Donovan, something that he couldn't put his finger on. He worked on first impressions and for the most part it had always served him well. Kane's mind drifted back to the day before....

The house he'd arrived at was well turned out and clearly looked after and much larger than anywhere he'd ever lived himself. The garden had looked almost as if it were being prepared for a flower show, such an array of colour sprung from it in the beautiful sunshine, this, typical of the rainy British weather that had been displayed only a day before. There at the door stood Mr. Donovan, a man in his early fifties, smartly dressed leaning up against the door frame, seemingly without a care in the World. He'd telephoned Kane only the day previously to arrange to meet him. Usually he only met possible clients at the office, but this man had been insistent that he visit him. Donovan's desire to take Kane out of his safety zone was the first warning bell and right there he'd seriously considered turning the job down. He couldn't understand why the man had been so insistent he go to him. Kane could see why though as he walked down the garden path. Had he lived here he'd also be reluctant to venture to his living hell part of the town. Looking at the Monetesque garden, Kane instantly felt less fortunate. Mr Donovan smiled at Kane but only with his mouth, his eyes were vacant and elsewhere. He looked as though he was just using his body to exist in, internally he appeared practically dead. The relaxed assured man from a distance looked lethargic and devoid of any kind of confidence up close, as if each breath would surely be his last.

Kane held his hand out. "Terrence Kane" he said. Mr Donovan seemed to take an age to respond as he stared through Kane, with the same vacant expression, matched with his eerie smile. "Clarke Donovan" he replied, shaking Kane by the hand in a limp and unenthusiastic manner. "Please come through."

Donovan led Kane through a long hallway towards the living room. The hallway was lined with mirrors and pictures of equal number. Kane reflected throughout the length of the hall as he slowly ventured down it, thinking that he'd probably never seen so many mirrors outside of a travelling fair. His shoes squeaked on the wooden flooring with every step. The squeals of his footwear reverberating around him. The decor inside was old, even older than the man leading Kane down the hall.

"Lived here long?" Kane asked.

Donovan stopped for a brief moment, as if he was unable to walk and think at the same time. "All of my life, this place belonged to my parents, I grew up here."

Donovan began to walk again, leading Kane into the living room while pointing towards an old worn armchair, presumably for Kane to sit in rather than draw his attention to. It was old and threadbare and Kane worried it would collapse as he sat down, but it felt sturdier than it appeared when he finally did. The living room itself was walled in flock paper with a patterned brown carpet. Kane felt he could easily have walked straight into a scene from a seventies television series such was the authenticity of this decorating nightmare. "My wife is having an affair," Donovan said coldly, answering a question nobody had asked him.

"And you're sure?" Kane responded, linking the fingers of each hand together on his lap.

"Absolutely, I know, the signs are there," Donovan said, still standing. Kane thought for a short while. "Those signs may not be what you think they are Mr Donovan, have you actually tried speaking to your wife and asking her?"

"Of course I have, I'm not an idiot, however she does insist on treating me like one. I know she only married me for my money," Donovan responded, his face reddening with either embarrassment or anger.

"Well if she is having an affair Mr Donovan I will find out, of that you can be 100 percent assured" Kane replied, confidently.

"You don't look like a Private Eye," Donovan said.

"We don't all look like Phillip Marlowe and neither would we want to," Kane answered, smiling. Donovan still had that blank, almost cold expression. He handed an envelope to Kane.

"This is where she'll be today, at work, but then she'll be going to lunch and doing whatever it is she does with him." Donovan looked at Kane in a way that made him feel as if he was the one being accused. There was something odd about Donovan that Kane wasn't sure of. Everything he said and did seem scripted and pre-meditated. There was nothing natural about the way Donovan spoke and behaved and that unnerved Kane.

"Listen, if you're that sure, then you probably don't need me," Kane answered. "I wouldn't just take your money for the sake of it."

"NO!" Donovan snapped back before Kane had even finished his last word. "You don't understand Mr Kane, I do know what is going on, but I need to see it, I need the evidence, when I divorce her, she gets nothing, that bitch gets absolutely nothing!" Donovan spat this last word out with sheer unadulterated hatred and anger.

"I understand Mr Donovan," Kane said. "I'll do what you need."

"This is all my own fault Mr Kane," Donovan said. "She's twenty years my junior, I should have known this would happen." Kane wasn't sure what to say to this. He guessed, if that were the case, Donovan had really opened himself up to the possibility of something like this happening. He couldn't say so though. Kane looked at the picture of the pretty blonde he was holding and then looked at the hardened old face of Donovan. Yes, he really should have seen it coming.

He promised to let Donovan know as soon as he had some news, negative or otherwise and quickly made his way out of the house.

Walking away from the place, in the now humid and muggy daytime air, the whole area didn't feel as inviting as it had when he arrived. He looked back at the figure of Mr Donovan again, watching this time from the window.

He couldn't help feeling as though the air was trying to warn him of some kind of impending doom. The whole place felt creepy all of a sudden, out there in the middle of nowhere. What had appeared homely and inviting, the perfect retreat when he arrived was now the last place Kane wished to be. He craved the squalid familiarity of home. As he continued to retreat away from Donovan's house, he could almost feel the man's eyes piercing through the back of his skull.

Chapter Two

Sometimes, in fact most times, the job of a Private Eye was particularly boring, nothing like you see in the movies at all. Little fun and practically no adventure, just sitting around waiting and watching.

Kane sat in the driver seat of his car, the one place other than his flat, he spent most time. His car was, to all intents and purposes, his office. He'd situated himself outside Mrs Donovan's place of work just as he had been told to. Kane knew Donovan's wife was inside, innocently working away, unaware a man outside was preparing to blow her world apart. Kane sometimes found himself wracked with guilt. The time he spent alone in the car gave him ample and often unwanted opportunity to think. For all he knew Mr Donovan could be no more than a wife beating control freak. Mrs Donovan's extra curricular activity may well be her only source of enjoyment out of a miserable existence. However, Kane had to put those thoughts aside, Mr Donovan had employed him to do a job and it was his duty to fulfil that role, irrespective of whether he enjoyed it. Working as a Police Officer, Kane had fast learned, it was not enjoying the job which got the bills paid.

Kane looked down at the picture of the pretty blonde woman Donovan had given him. Mrs Donovan was extremely attractive and he couldn't help but wonder what the hell she was doing with a man like Donovan. It couldn't be money, if she was that well off she wouldn't still be working, looking at the interior of the house, it was hardly screaming wealth from every wall. Relationships, although seemingly intense and real at the time did, invariably turn stagnant and routine. Kane expected that was the reason behind Mrs Donovan's fall from grace, as opposed to anything else.

Kane sat there reading a paper, enlightening himself with endless stories of how the world and especially the country, were in total turmoil and on their way to capitulation, if you believe the scaremongering press.

He wondered how Mrs Donovan would feel if she were to know a man was sitting outside her place of work waiting for her to make a wrong move. He wondered how he would feel if it happened to him. Not happy, he surmised, but then who the hell would want to watch him? There really wasn't anybody interested enough in what was going on with Terrence Kane, little ever was.

Before too long Mrs Donovan made her way out of the building. Kane looked at his watch, the time had just gone past one in the afternoon so he guessed she was presumably off to lunch. She walked along the high street continuing her journey for around five minutes, oblivious to him, slowly following her on foot. He watched her graceful movements along the pavement. Hardly a man she passed failed to notice her. She would stand out in any crowd. Kane had decided trailing her in the car could well turn out to be a wrong move, just in case she took an alleyway or a short cut he couldn't get down. The whole town was littered in one-way streets and following by car could often prove to be a hindrance rather than a help.

That had happened to him before, tailing a young guy who'd been suspected of filtering away money from his company's bank accounts. Something as simple as an alleyway proved to be a real bugbear for a vehicle encased Private Eye.

After a short while of walking Mrs Donovan stopped outside a candle shop where she was met by a towering black man, probably 6ft 5" at least. His girth alone doubled Kane's size and he involuntarily stepped back a bit, his natural instinct turning towards self preservation. Kane looked at the man, he was three times the size of Donovan. He also guessed the man was likely to cause him considerable injury if he spotted him. The job required an element of risk sometimes and he knew he'd have to take a chance if he intended on getting a good shot of the two of them together.

As Mrs Donovan lent forward to kiss the man, Kane was perfectly poised to catch the moment forever in a digital frame.

Still unaware, the two walked off, closely followed by Kane, who now had a shot of them holding hands. So far so good and possibly the easiest money he had made since taking on his freelance position. There had been little chasing around apart from a few hours staking out the office block, he had not had to wait long for a result. Mrs Donovan and the large black man made their way into a seedy looking motel with its red neon sign flashing in the daylight above. Any uncertainty Kane had about these two evaporated in that instant. Figuring they were not there to admire the decor or make the beds, Kane captured another snapshot of his prey, as they made their way through the entrance of motel seedy. He watched them retreat inside, completely unaware of his presence and how he'd taken a storyboard of pictures, ready to unveil them to this week's paying customer.

It was here that the job became extra difficult. Getting photos of the two on their way to this rendezvous had been easy, but completing the ultimate goal of capturing them in the act, that was going to take some well worn skill, or some fantastic luck.

Kane looked at the side of the building and spotted the fire escape. Looking up the side of the building he could clearly see four rooms that, should he want to, he'd be able to peer straight into.

He looked at the small size of the motel and decided that the odds were good that Mrs Donovan would indeed be in one of those rooms. Of course it was equally as likely they wouldn't be either.

He made his way over to the stainless-steel fire escape. The heavy rain from earlier sat in small puddles on each uneven and slightly slippery step.

He knew his luck had been in so far today, but couldn't help but admit the possibility of slipping and breaking his neck on these stairs was probably likely. "It's meant to be a fire escape," he said to himself. "You'd probably break your neck coming down the thing," he said again, talking quietly so as not to look like yet another of the towns randomly talking aloud head cases.

He slowly clambered up the apparently unsafe stairs. It wasn't as slippery or dangerous as he'd visualised, but the metal was surprisingly cold to the touch, despite the stifled heat of the day.

As he approached the first window he could hear noises. Peering in, the curtain was open. He could see two figures in the room, not deterred by his movement at all, they were too busy focusing on themselves. Neither figure in the room was Mrs Donovan or her tall, dark stranger, at least Kane hoped neither of the people he was looking at were. Whatever they were doing, it looked painful and although one of the participants was black, they weren't naturally black.

Onwards to the second window, Kane was disappointed to see the curtains had been closed. Whether there was anyone in there he didn't know, but he figured there was a good chance that Mrs Donovan could well be behind that curtain covered pane. If that was the case then he'd have to revert to the dreaded plan B. He'd only used plan B twice before and both times had almost got him killed. It was a simple case of deduction. Once worked out which room his photo shoot was to take place he'd do the following. Firstly, kick the door open and secondly take some quick shots before running, quickly. The two occasions Kane had done this resulted in him being chased down the corridors by a naked man Some people really had no shame.

Kane decided to move on and check the other two windows before resorting to such drastic measures, sure that Mrs Donovan would ultimately be in the room with the drawn curtains.

He was wrong. In the third room, windows and curtains open, there was Mrs Donovan, doing something with the large black man that was definitely not what she'd gone to work to do this morning. He took some more photos of the two, both so wrapped up in each other he was pretty sure he could walk straight up to them and get some close ups without being spotted. In fact, the black man was so engrossed, Kane guessed he could get him to sign one of the photos as well.

He didn't do this of course; he didn't need to. he finished taking his photo's, observing that the black guy wasn't big all over. "Maybe its not true what they say" he thought to himself, as he made his way down the stairs, careful not to slip.

Back at the car he called Mr Donovan and told him he had something for him to see. Donovan wanted to know more but Kane assured him it was something he'd be better off showing him face to face. Hanging up the phone on a frustrated sounding

Clarke Donovan, he made his way home, to print the evidence and take it to his client.

A couple of hours later Kane had the photos printed and ready to show Mr Donovan. They'd come out well, maybe too well, but Donovan was a paying customer and he had to show him exactly what he had paid for. It wasn't pretty and this part of the job was often the most distressing for Kane, but he knew it had to be done, he hoped it would be enough to at least give Donovan back some control over his life.

He packed the photos into his inside pocket and made his way back down to his car, ready to take the journey to Mr Donovan's house again, hopefully for the final time.

Kane congratulated himself in his head, it was a good job well done. Easy, but well done all the same

As he strapped himself into the car and started the ignition, he noticed the sky again looked heavy, he guessed the heavens would open just as he took the walk down Donovan's long driveway. Still, he consoled himself with the knowledge that so far today he'd been exceptionally lucky and was about to get paid for his good fortune.

Lightening split the sky and thunder filled the air as Kane arrived in the exterior woodland of Donovan's humble abode.

Large drops of rain hit the windscreen of the car like balls of silver, rolling into his eye line until eventually he gave in and turned on the wipers.

Parking nearer than before, but still far enough away to get quite wet, Kane stopped the car and sat, motionless. He loved the smell of the earth as the rain hit, that aroma of dirt and life filling the air and invading his senses. The rain became quite heavy as the thunder grew louder and more menacing, shattering the stillness above. Kane had always been fascinated by the quiet eeriness before the crack of thunder, the animals in the surrounding areas knowingly hiding from the storm before it had arrived.

As he emerged from the car he could clearly see the lights on in the Donovan household and was fairly sure he could also see Donovan's silhouette standing in the window.

Kane made his way down the driveway and despite it still being only 4pm the sky was black, almost as though it had prematurely turned to night. He reached the front door of Clarke Donovan's household, soaking wet, but for his hood protected head. Knocking loudly, he waited silently while the sky around him continued to erupt and boom in protest.

The door opened and there stood Donovan. Kane could instantly smell the alcohol on his breath and was relatively sure that a lighted match just about now could well cause an explosion.

"Come in" said Donovan in a vague and distant voice. Kane said nothing but followed the deliberately slow man down the mirrored hall. He could sense Donovan was drunk enough to stumble but sober enough to concentrate on his walking. He was probably still a drink or two away from passing out. This for Kane had always been a 'danger' phase. The time when he would most likely act stupidly, behave like a total idiot and invariably hurt or offend someone. But he rarely drunk these days. He'd never been entirely sure whether he suffered a drink problem or not, but felt that his inability to control it while he was actually consuming alcohol constituted a problem of sorts and so, decided not to drink too often. He'd drink alone, but not with company, because alone all he could hurt was himself and he was thick skinned enough to take his own insults, internal or otherwise.

Donovan pointed to the same chair as before and sat in the one opposite.

Sitting down, Kane began to speak. "I'm afraid I have what you wanted," he said, as Donovan looked on with his drunken gaze.

"What was that?" he replied in a slightly slurred manner.

Kane wasn't sure what was meant by this, bearing in mind it was Donovan who had sent him off to get the evidence he needed in the first place.

"The photos you asked for, some conclusive proof," he replied, before passing the envelope to Donovan. He took the envelope but did not immediately open it. Instead, he continued to look at Kane, no longer with the lifeless, vacant smile, but with those equally void eyes.

"Do you like it?" He said to Kane. "Like what?" Kane thought to himself, unsure where this was going. "I don't understand what you mean Mr Donovan, do I like what?" Kane said, slightly unnerved by Donovan's continued blank expression.

"Do you like your job Mr Kane, does it fulfil you, embalm your life with richness?" Donovan said, still completely focussing on Kane and not on the envelope in his hand, the envelope which contained the answers he'd seemed desperate for only the day before.

"No," Kane replied, "It most certainly does not Mr Donovan, but it does, whichever way you look at it, pay the bills, which at the end of the day is all any of us work for. If we didn't need the money we wouldn't do it" Donovan continued to look at Kane until eventually cracking his pose with a smile.

"Indeed Mr Kane, indeed" he replied. "I doubt there is a single person in this world who would work for a living unless they absolutely needed to," Donovan responded. "Work is not life, it's a necessity of life, as well as a preventative to it, wouldn't you agree Mr Kane?". Kane looked at him, wondering to himself exactly what Donovan was going on about. "Are you going to open the envelope Mr Donovan?" He asked. "It is after all, what you are paying me for. "Of course, of course" said Donovan. "How silly of me to assume you'd come here for anything else; you want to see a broken man don't you?" Kane was disturbed by Donovan's phrasing. He did not always like being the messenger as more often than not his client would shoot him down with misplaced blame.

"Absolutely not Mr Donovan, I want to get paid and get the fuck out of here. I've done my bit, now its time to do yours," Kane responded, bluntly, not wanting an awkward conversation.

Donovan's eyes briefly flickered over Kane's face before resting on the envelope. With slow assuredness, he opened the envelope, tearing carefully as if the last flower on earth remained inside and he must do his utmost to preserve it. Eventually Donovan opened the padded brown envelope and removed the photos inside. He seemed to take an age to look at them, examining each one as though he were looking for some evidence they had been falsified.

"Well," he said. "That's interesting isn't it? You certainly got some fun out of this job eh?" Kane looked at the back of the photos. "I get no pleasure from this, in fact I find it seedy and a little repellent," he replied.

"I bet you do," said Donovan, "Its like free porn isn't it, watching those people have sex while you take photos? Did you get into this job because you are a voyeur Mr Kane, or did the job make you one?" Donovan sniped.

"I got into this job because I could no longer work as a Detective, Mr Donovan, so I used the best of my abilities to make a career elsewhere. Like I say, its not enjoyable, but it pays the bills". Kane was getting a little pissed at Donovan's attitude, it wasn't his fault the guy's wife was screwing around, if anything it was Donovan's.

"I'll tell you what I hate the most, shall I" said Donovan.

"About me?" enquired Kane.

Donovan laughed at this. "No, about this" he responded, pointing to the photos. "It sickens me that it had to be a nigger, I mean, of all people she could have let put a cock in her, it had to be a coon didn't it. I feel physically sick to be honest with you Mr Kane." said Donovan.

Kane was taken aback by the coldness of Donovan's statement. "I don't subscribe to your racism Mr Donovan and to be fair, this is something you need to discuss with your wife, not me."

Donovan raised his eyes at this "Sorry, another one of the PC brigade are we? No wonder this country is fucked"

Kane was no longer in the mood for these games and as a loud crack of thunder erupted he rose from is chair. "Listen Mr Donovan, I've done my part, now pay me so I can go and you can have this discussion with your wife," "Fair enough" replied Donovan as he stood up. "I'll see you out Mr Kane, thank you so much for all your hard work". He finished the last sentence with a sarcastic undertone, not unnoticed by Kane.

The two men made their way back down the corridor and approached the front door.

"I need my payment Mr Donovan" Kane said as Donovan made a move to turn the front door handle.

"Of course, of course you do. Will this be enough?" he asked, as he pulled a gun out of his belt behind him.

"What are you doing?" Kane said in a fearful tone.

"Paying you Mr Kane" said Donovan as he fired two shots directly into Kane's chest. In searing, burning pain, before he could even realise what had happened, Kane sunk to the floor, watching the reflection of his blood-stained chest in one of the many walled mirrors. Struggling to intake breath and woozy from the lack of oxygen, Kane had enough time to witness Donovan blow his brains all over one of the mirrors and collapse to the floor, before he himself passed out.

Chapter Three

"Mr Kane, Mr Kane," whispered the voice. Suddenly the dark behind Terrence Kane's eyes was invaded by the searing light prizing its way between them. "Mr Kane" the soft voice of the woman said again, practically whispering.

Slowly opening his eyes, feeling his lashes pull apart from encrustation, Kane felt the light pour in, shattering his brain with blistering pulsating bursts. He felt like he'd never seen light so bright, his entire head hurt from the enormity of it. His temples throbbed intensely. Gradually adjusting to the light, he realised he was lying in a bed, but one which was not familiar to him.

"Mr Kane, it's good to see you awake Sir," said the woman's voice, slightly more audible than before.

His eyes adjusted further and he could make out the blurred silhouette of a person standing there in the light, which was now no longer so strong.

"Who are you?" he asked, with a croaky dry voice, almost indistinguishable as his own.

"I'm your Nurse Mr Kane" she replied. He lie still for a short while still trying to focus on the woman.

"So I'm in hospital?" he responded, his voice still sounding as though it belonged to someone else.

"As far as I'm aware, there are no Nurses anywhere else Mr Kane" she replied.

"What's happened to me, how long have I been here?" he asked her.

"You were shot Mr Kane," she answered. "You sustained some heavy damage, you've been in intensive care for the past two weeks, it's been fifty-fifty all the way, but you're here now, eyes open, so I guess you've made it."

Kane lay still trying to recall what had happened to him and then slowly he remembered Donovan and the shooting. In the space of five seconds, Kane went from knowing nothing to remembering absolutely everything.

"What is your name?" he asked the nurse.

"I'm Jane," she responded, "Jane Henderson". Kane's sight began to improve and he could make her out in her uniform. She was short, with brown hair and a pleasant face.

"How did I get here?" he asked her. "I was alone, I was out in the middle of nowhere."

"You was not alone Mr Kane" she said, "I don't think you were ever alone".

"Well no, I guess I wasn't completely alone, otherwise I wouldn't have been shot, but the man who shot me, I remember, he then shot himself, I remember that clearly" said Kane.

"That's right" she said, "He did, he killed himself, but his wife turned up in time to call an ambulance."

"Really, she called an ambulance?" Kane said. "She had no reason to call an ambulance for me, I'm the reason her husband killed himself".

Nurse Henderson laughed at this. "Don't be silly Mr Kane, he shot himself out of choice, we pieced together what happened from speaking to her, she realised what had happened when she saw the photos Mr Kane, she saved you".

At that point the door opened and Kane, eyesight fully restored, could see a tall man in a Doctors white coat, standing there in the doorway.

"Nurse Henderson, please leave the room while I talk to the patient" he said.

Nurse Henderson quickly left the room and left Kane alone with the Doctor.

"Good Morning Mr Kane" he said, in a deep rasping voice, which echoed around Kane's head. "How are you feeling this morning?" he asked.

"I've been better," he said "But I've been worse as well".

The Doctor laughed at this. "You're not wrong Mr Kane, we thought we'd never see you here, it was close for awhile, but now we've arrived at this point and you must be pleased"? he said.

"I am Doctor, extremely, I knew it was bad when he shot me but exactly how bad was it?" Kane asked.

"As bad as it could be, bullets in the chest aren't easy to get over I'm afraid, but you've almost made it to the other side now and we're very pleased with you, it was a long time coming, you really put up a fight." the Doctor said.

"That's great news," he replied. "Any ideas of the time then?"

"Its really up to you" said the Doctor. "I'm sure you will know when you are ready to move on, but right now, I'd suggest you get some rest and take each moment as it comes".

"Thank you Doc" said Kane, "Thank you for everything".

"It's my job to take care of you Mr Kane, that's what I'm here for, don't thank me." he said.

"You didn't tell me your name" said Kane.

"Sorry, how rude of me, I'm Dr Hedtolg" replied the Doctor.

"Doctor Hedtolg, not a very English name, yet you sound very local, if you don't mind me saying" said Kane.

"Ever the Detective Mr Kane" said the Doctor, "My Father was Norwegian, my Mother on the other hand, she's a born and bred Londoner, my first name is Rodney!" laughed the Doctor.

"Now that's a proper name Mr Hedtolg" laughed Kane.

"You can call me Rod" said the Doctor.

"You can call me Terrence" smiled Kane.

"Get some rest now Terrence" said the Doctor, "You'll need as much as possible before you go back to being a full time Detective and not just a hospital one!"

"I think after recent events I need a career change" said Kane, as Doctor Hedtolg opened the door to leave.

"Don't let recent events put you off Mr Kane, by all accounts, I understand you are good at what you do" Doctor Hedtolg said.

"Maybe, but I don't really want to go through anything like this again, I should have gone with my gut feeling and left that case alone" Kane responded.

"If you were unhappy Mr Kane you should have trusted your gut feeling, they are rarely wrong you know" Doctor Hedtolg said. "It's our guardian angels trying to point us in the right direction."

Kane smiled at this. He thought about answering but, despite his recent extended rest, still felt tired. A full blown conversation about his beliefs, or lack of them, was not on the current agenda.

"I guess so Doctor" Kane said in response. Doctor Hedtolg smiled.

"Well I'm sure once you're out of here your passion for being a Detective will re awaken" Doctor Hedtolg said. "Once a detective always a detective." he said, as he closed the door quietly behind him. Kane was already asleep before it finally clicked into place.

Kane lay in the bed staring at the matt white ceiling. He'd really come that close to death, surprisingly so. He'd not been too sure about Donovan from the start. Hedtolg was right, he should have gone with his instincts, it's what had made him a good, no great, detective in the past yet ignoring them had almost got him killed.

He felt angry with Donovan, if it wasn't for him he wouldn't be here and at the end of the day it was Donovan who had employed him, Donovan who had asked him to spy on his wife and Donovan who had wanted to hear what Kane had told him.

Fair enough, if he decided to kill his wife, she probably deserved it, if he chose to kill himself, then fine as well, not Kane's problem, but shooting him had been unprovoked and unwarranted.

As he lay there reflecting, he realised had it not been for Mrs Donovan he'd be dead now as well. He wondered, had she seen the photo's first, the evidence that had led to the blood bath she had returned home to, would she be so quick to pick up that phone and call the ambulance for him? He guessed he'd never know.

Kane had been serious about giving up the Detective work. He'd been secretly sick of it for a while now. It caused so much hurt and pain to others, fairly regularly and now it had caused so much personal harm to him, he really did think enough was enough. Time to move on, but go where? That he hadn't decided, but he knew he needed a change of scenery. Looking out of his window, the rain again poured down the panes of glass. He wondered if it had been raining as long as he'd been in intensive care, knowing England, it probably had.

'Intensive Care,' thought Kane, that really was bad, the closest to death he'd ever been. He guessed that having worked in the police force for so long and in a failing society, he'd been lucky up until now. He had given up believing in God a long time ago, figuring that if he believed he was just going to die and be no more, then if anything really did exist after death, it would be a bonus. By thinking like this, he had nothing to lose.

He realised though, for the first time, how sure he felt, he'd been in intensive care for two weeks and could think of not one instance during that time that he would say he'd had a so called 'near death' experience. He'd heard so many stories in the past and wondered if in the same situation he'd get his epiphany, but he didn't. Kane wasn't overly concerned, but had he some kind of paranormal near death experience during that time it would at least have been the ultimate detective work!

Instead, he settled for quiet recuperation. It could have been so much worse after all.

Chapter Four

The three boys wandered close to the edge of the train track, tentatively looking in each direction to see if there was anything coming. They were all around twelve years of age, but that was where the similarity ended. The first boy was tall with dark hair, the second boy short with blonde hair and the third boy between both in height, but chubby with ginger hair.

"Brian Mackeson told me his cousin was standing by a train track and he got sucked right under the train as it flew past, his body got sliced up into millions of pieces" said the ginger boy.

"You're an idiot" said the dark haired boy. "You'll believe anything"

"I'm not an idiot" said the ginger boy, "I'm telling you it happened, his cousin was all over the track. They buried him in a shoe box."

The other two boys laughed and ran across the track to the other side, leaving the ginger boy still deciding whether to go or not.

"Are you coming or not, chicken." said the blonde boy.

"I'm not a chicken all right, I just don't want to get bloody squished." The other two laughed again.

The track, lined with trees on either side, could easily be missed, but the sound of the approaching train could not. All three boys looked up the track to see a train there, waiting for the red light.

"OK, wait until this one has come past and then come over, we don't have all day Harvey." said the dark haired boy.

"OK, you two why don't you just sit over there in the tree," said Harvey. "Terry and Christopher sitting in a tree K-I-S-S-I-N-G" he continued. "You're such a card" said the blonde boy. "Now stand back, you don't want to get sucked under the train" the two boys laughed again.

"Piss off Chris." Harvey responded.

"Ooooh he said a bad word." said Chris. The other kid, Terry, laughed. "Don't worry Harvey" said Terry. "There's no way a train will suck your fat arse into it."

"Better not do, he'd derail it." Chris said, leaving both himself and Terry doubled over with laughter. The train began to approach at speed.

Harvey stood back even further and tried to make out the faces of the passengers as the train hurtled past. As quickly as that the train was gone. Harvey looked ahead to where his friends had been standing. "Guys, where are you?" he asked. There was no answer. "Seriously guys, where are you?" still he was met with stony silence. Harvey slowly made his way across the track, now no longer looking in either direction but focusing on the spot where his friends had been standing. Neither Terry or Chris were anywhere to be seen. "Guys." he said again. Starting to breathe heavily. Harvey was beginning to fear the worse. He went back to the track, to check for signs of bodies and could have sworn he saw blood on the tracks. "Oh God," he said under his breath, "Oh God, they've been run over, Oh God, Oh God, what am I going to do?" all of a sudden Harvey started crying and was then shaken out of it by the sound of "Boo!" as the two boys jumped out from behind a tree, very nearly scaring the life out of Harvey.

"Screw you guys", he said. "That's not bloody funny, piss off". Chris and Terry were doubled over again, laughing hysterically.

"I think you wet yourself." Chris said to Harvey.

"I think I'm gonna wet myself!" Terry said, laughing uncontrollably. After a few more seconds of the two boys composing themselves, they all got ready to venture on.

"How much further is it?" Harvey asked after a short while, "My Mum wants me home by six." Terry looked at his watch. "Don't worry, its only eleven thirty, we're about another half hour away, it'll be good fun when we get there and I have a little surprise as well."

The other two looked eager at this news, Terry was good at surprises. Neither of them pushed to know what it was though, they knew better than that, he'd never tell them anyway. The sun beat down strongly on the tops of their heads as the boys continued their journey across the large field and all three of them stopped to take a flask out of the small bags on there backs.

"It's really hot out here." said Harvey, taking a swig from his flask.

"Sun don't like the ginger's does it." said Chris, laughing.

"I'm not ginger, it's strawberry blonde" said Harvey, much to the amusement of the other two. "Yeah" said Terry, "Only strawberries aren't orange coloured, otherwise they'd be called oranges."

After their short drink break, the three boys began to walk again. At the same time all of them noticed a man, halfway down the field, in the middle of it, he seemed to be coming their way. He was walking with real purpose.

"Who's that?" asked Harvey. Neither Chris or Terry said a thing. All three turned to look at each other

"What if it's him?" said Chris.

"Who?" said Terry.

Harvey was as white as a sheet and shaking.

"Jesus, he means the guy who murdered Sally White, it could be as well couldn't it?" Chris said, beginning to share Harvey's appearance. Terry laughed, nervously. "Sally White is missing, not dead, she might not be dead at all".

It was clear to all three the man walking towards them had increased his speed and was not very happy either. He appeared to be shaking his hand at them.

"Run." said Terry.

"Which way?" said Chris.

"Just follow me." Terry replied

All of a sudden Terry took off in the direction they had been walking, but at a pace and with Harvey and Chris closely following. For a chubby little thing Harvey sure could run when his adrenaline was pumping and he thought he was about to become a murderers next victim.

The man who had been making his way towards them ran after them, shouting something that none of them recognised, although Harvey was pretty sure it was "I'm going to kill you"!

Running so hard their chests burned with pain they eventually came to the edge of the field and road. Crossing it without taking any care at all, they found their way to the entrance of a dirt track, which looked as though it led up a path and into some woodland.

The man who had been chasing them stood on the edge of the field now, hands on hips and breathing heavily, looking across the road at them. "Stay off my land," he shouted, before turning around and making his way back across the field.

"It was the bloody farmer!," Harvey said and they all fell about laughing this time, Terry laying on the ground, through a mixture of laughter and exhaustion.

"Well guys" he said, when he finally caught his breath, "We've just shaved fifteen minutes off our journey time, we only need to make it up this track and we're there."

Once the boys had recovered their breath and the burning in their chests had eased up, they got started on their journey again, making their way up the lonely and dusty dirt track.

None of them said much on the way, they all felt a mixture of excitement at the day ahead and terror at what had happened. None of them were about to admit they thought they were about to be murdered, but all three of them had been thinking exactly the same thing.

"I didn't think we would be able to outrun that guy," Harvey said, amazed at his own ability to pick up speed when he thought his life depended on it.

"I was just making sure I outran you," Chris replied.

Finally they reached the end of the dirt track. Sitting there at the end was a small wooden gate which all three of them easily climbed over.

"You sure this isn't private land as well?" asked Harvey.

"No, my Dad used to bring me up here all the time" said Terry. "We used to come over and fly kites." Terry was gazing off into the distance, thinking of a time long ago.

"Kites" said Harvey "That's a bit babyish." Chris punched him on the top of the arm. "Ouch, why did you do that?" he asked.

"Because you're an idiot," said Chris.

Harvey looked at Terry realising what he had just said.

"You miss your Dad Terry?" he asked

"Yeah Harv, every day." Looking down at the ground, Terry quickly changed the subject. "Want to see what I brought with me?" he said. Neither Chris or Harvey needed asking twice. "Look at this" said Terry, opening his bag. The three boys all carefully peered in together as if a dangerous animal would jump out.

"No way!" Chris and Harvey said together.

Terry smiled. "Oh yes"

Chapter Five

Kane awoke with a start. Blearily looking around at his surroundings briefly forgetting where he was. "Hi" said a deep voice next to him he didn't recognise. Kane looked to his left and there in the bed to his left lay a man. The guy was in his fifties, greying hair and a tired face.

"Hi there" said Kane. "Where did you come from?".

The guy smiled. "They wheeled me in here earlier, you were dead to the world my man". He stopped for a second and then said. "I'm Harry Leadbitter"

"Hi Harry, nice to meet you" Kane said. "I'm Terrence Kane".

"I know," said Leadbitter, they told me your story.

"Really?" replied Kane. "Who's they?"

Leadbitter laughed again. "THEY are the reason you're here. Sounds to me like you are a very lucky man," he continued.

Kane couldn't disagree with that. "Yes, yes I am, very, guess it wasn't my time." Leadbitter looked on.

"Maybe not, it seems your guardian angel was looking down on you Mr Kane."

It was Kane's turn to laugh. "Yes, if you believe in all that, I'm more inclined to believe the Doctors did a bloody good job and they saved my life."

"You don't believe in Angels then Mr Kane?" asked Leadbitter.

"I believe in Newton and Hawking and because of that I can't really believe in Angels. Call me Terrence as well, I don't like being called Mr Kane."

Leadbitter didn't say anything for a short while and Kane wasn't sure if he'd just finished speaking for now. Suddenly, Leadbitter spoke again. "I guess everybody is entitled to believe in what they wish eh? I mean the World would be a boring place if we all believe in the same thing wouldn't it?" he said.

"Maybe so Mr Leadbitter, but it would probably be a safer place as well" Kane replied.

Leadbitter again went quiet, seeming to ponder Kane's statement. "How do you mean?" he finally said.

Kane tried to take as long as Leadbitter to say anything, but couldn't wait to offer his opinion again. "Well to be fair, if it wasn't for religion we'd probably have next to no war at all. Most of the Worlds conflicts are over religion and wouldn't the World be a better place without it?" Kane said. He felt fairly pleased with himself. He was and always had been a completely devoted atheist and he enjoyed stamping all over peoples beliefs.

Once again, Leadbitter was quietly thinking. "You have a point Terrence, you have a point, I guess the only way we'll ever really find out is when we die." Leadbitter said.

Kane was getting bored of the conversation. Having been that close to death, he was pretty fed up with talking about it. He wondered what Leadbitter was doing in there and decided it was time to find out, after all he seemed to have a head start on Kane before he'd even woken up.

"Why are you in here anyway?" Kane asked.

Leadbitter looked puzzled "I said they wheeled me in here while you was sleeping". he replied.

"I mean, why are you in here, what's wrong with you?" Kane said, widely gesturing with his hands to signify he meant 'in the hospital'.

"Cancer" Leadbitter said. "Colon cancer"

Kane looked at him. He looked remarkably well considering and Kane figured he wasn't long into the illness. "Early stage I take it?" Kane asked.

Leadbitter shook his head in a grave and final way. "Far from it, when I first found out, that seems like another lifetime it was so long ago. I'm as near to the end as I'm going to be" Leadbitter said.

Kane didn't know how to respond to that, Leadbitter had been so calm and collected when he said that. Kane figured he was just resigned to the fact his days were numbered.

"I'm sorry," Kane said. "That's pretty shitty and you look so well, I figured you had a fighting chance".

"Don't apologise" Leadbitter said "I guess looks are deceiving." Kane nodded his head in understanding.

"I apologise for shitting all over religion and your beliefs as well, I wasn't trying to do that. I guess right now, what you believe is important to you?" Kane said.

"Yes it is of course, very, but then it always has been," Leadbitter replied. "I'm not using my death as an excuse to believe in God and the afterlife now, I always have done."

Kane appreciated a man with the courage of his convictions and for the next few minutes, neither of them said anything, they both just looked at the ceiling. The silence was not at all uncomfortable. Eventually it was Kane who spoke again.

"Do you ever read much into your dreams?" he asked.

Leadbitter thought for a moment. "Why, how do you mean, read much into them?" he responded.

"Well, I had this dream earlier," Kane said. "It was a mirror image of something that happened to me as a kid. It played out in my head exactly as it played out that day. I could feel and smell everything I felt on the day, what do you think about that?" he asked Leadbitter.

"What was the dream about?" Leadbitter asked.

Kane went on to tell him the whole story, from the train, to the joke on Harvey, the man in the field, the chase, right up to the point he'd woken up.

"That's strange," Leadbitter said. "Does it mean anything to you?" Kane wasn't sure if it was meant to be significant or just an odd dream. Perhaps it meant nothing and had been purely that, just a dream, a re-run of something long ago, but the vividness of it had really hit him and he couldn't explain why. Kane had heard of people having flash backs when they were close to death, but not after they'd survived, but that was exactly what it had felt like, a flashback.

Later that evening, while both were sleeping, Kane was again awoken with a start, but this time by something moving in the room. With all the lights off and natural light now replaced by total darkness, it was practically impossible to see anything at all. Again, he heard movement, a sound in the corner perhaps.

"Leadbitter?" Kane asked. Questioning whether it was Leadbitter moving, his answer was in the form of a loud snore. Clearly it was not Leadbitter moving, not while sleeping that loudly!

Kane rolled onto his side and again felt as though something was moving in the room. He decided to try and go back to sleep as it was more than likely his mind was just playing tricks on him. He closed his eyes and was just about to drift off again when, like the sound of a faint breeze, he heard a whisper.

"Paaaahhhhh" it seemed to say.

He lay very still, hardly breathing at all, trying to listen intently to the sound.

Again, it came, this time over to the right corner of the room. "Faaaahhhhh Paaaaahhhhh."

Kane's blood felt as though it had turned to ice. He was shaking. Whatever it was, it was right there in the room. Suddenly, the sound came again, only this time directly in his ear. He could feel breath, as cold as snow, he could hear the same senseless words. "Jesus Christ!" he screamed.

Leadbitter shot out of bed and threw the light on. "What's the matter?" he asked.

Kane's face was deathly white. "Did you hear that?" he asked Leadbitter.

"Hear what?" he asked.

"There was a noise, a whispering, it was bloody freezing in here, it whispered in my ear, right in my fucking ear!" Kane exclaimed.

Leadbitter started to laugh.

"What whispered in your ear?" he said.

"Christ knows, something, something did."

Leadbitter stopped laughing "Ok, suppose something did whisper in your ear, what the hell did it say?"

Kane lay in bed looking drained and slightly confused. "It said "Fahh pahh. What the bloody hell does that mean"?

"It doesn't mean anything you fool," said Leadbitter. "You were probably dreaming, go back to sleep". He turned the light off and got back into bed.

Kane continued to lay still, listening, but the sound did not return.

Chapter Six

The rain poured down again, in it's endless downward spiral, just as it had seemed to, ever since Kane had woken to find himself in the hospital. British weather was notoriously bad. Global warming had brought to Britain exactly the opposite, but even so, the current levels of rain were unprecedented. Kane sat in an office, lined with book cases, filled with books, mostly about medicine and the medical profession but within them, he spied a few classics. Lord of the Flies, Wuthering Heights and The Mayor of Casterbridge stood out amongst the Medical Encyclopaedia and it's related journals.

Dr Hedtolg walked into the room and sat down opposite Kane, smiling. "How are you feeling today Terrence?" he enquired, raising his eyebrows slightly.

"I feel fine" said Kane, "Right as rain in fact. The pain has practically gone and the physiotherapy has got 95% of my mobility back, I feel ready to go".

"Hmm, I see," said Hedtolg, "what about the voices?" he asked.

"The voices?" said Kane, slightly confused, "I don't hear any voices, I don't know what you're talking about."

Dr Hedtolg smiled. "Yes the voices, the whispering, the sounds which you have been hearing over the past few weeks, the sounds which, if you don't mind me saying, lead to Mr Leadbitter having to be moved out of your room." said Dr Hedtolg, still smiling.

"He told me he hadn't heard them, had never heard them." said Kane, confused.

"He didn't hear them Mr Kane," Dr Hedtolg replied, "He couldn't sleep though, with your nightly carrying on, that is why we had to move him, you were driving him crazy!" Hedtolg said, still smiling.

"Well that may be so" said Kane, angrily, "but I know what I am hearing and it is definitely there, I'm not making this bloody stuff up."

"Indeed," said Dr Hedtolg, suggesting he didn't actually believe Kane at all. "What is it the noises are making, or saying, as you put it?" he said this last part in a sarcastic almost mocking way.

"Faaahhh Paaahh" he replied, "It's a whisper, it's there nightly, whether you want to believe it or not, something sounds as if it wants to speak to me"

Hedtolg laughed at this. "Something Terrence, something like a ghost, you mean?"

"Well, no, not exactly, something unexplained." said Kane. He knew where Hedtolg was going. Dr Hedtolg was aware of Kane's beliefs and his denial in anything God like and he knew that admitting it might actually be a ghost, kind of contradicted what he said he believed in. Although he was aware of all these things and how they made him look a bit of a hypocrite, there was no getting away from the fact the sound he heard sounded ghostly and frightening. He didn't like it, but at the same time, felt it was trying to tell him something he had to know.

"It's probably just my imagination," Kane said, backtracking. "I've been in here a while now and I'm not used to being cooped up in the same place. It's some kind of cabin fever, if you like." he felt as though he needed to leave now, it was time to go, the hospital had done well in not only saving him but assisting him in a full recovery. For that, he'd be forever grateful, but he had a new life to begin, one away from being a Private Detective and one he was eager to get started.

"OK" said Dr Hedtolg, "You may well have a valid point there, it is feasible that your mind has been playing tricks on you. You suffered a major trauma and an indisputable shock. Shock can manifest itself in all kinds of ways and maybe this is it." Kane felt happy with this, it was after all a reasonable explanation, he had been close to death and there are few things more shocking than that.

"When can I go?" asked Kane.

Hedtolg laughed. "Used us for your needs and then tossing us out with the rubbish eh Terrence, I don't see any reason why you can't leave tomorrow, if you promise to make sure you keep up with your daily physio, even if you practice it yourself. It's important for your future well being" Dr Hedtolg said.

"Why can't I leave today?" asked Kane, impatiently itching to get out right away.

"I think you should spend one more night here, try and get through it without hearing any noises Terrence. Last chance to prove we don't need to release you from here and transfer you straight to the psychiatric ward" Dr Hedtolg said, laughing.

Kane reached across the desk and held out his hand, which Hedtolg took with a firm grip.

"Thank you so much Doctor for everything you and your staff have done for me, I will not forget it." he said.

"Don't thank us" said Hedtolg, "We were just there as your stop gap, between journeys, if you like and we're glad we could help you. Apart from your nightly ramblings you have been a fuss free patient. Our favourites".

Kane slowly rose from the chair, ready to leave and walked over to the door. "I intend for my next journey, to be something special as well" he said.

Hedtolg raised his eyebrows again. "Have you decided what you are going to do now you no longer want to be a Detective?" Dr Hedtolg asked him.

"No idea what I want to do. I just know what it is I don't want to do. We'll see which way the wind blows." he said.

"Good choice, but don't cut off your livelihood completely" Hedtolg answered. "You never know when you may next need it."

"I'll always be a detective in here," he said, pointing to his head, "But no longer in here." he continued, pointing to his chest.

"Just be careful, Mr Kane, whatever you do". Hedtolg said "Whatever path you think you have laid out before you, invariably ends up taking you somewhere completely unexpected.

Kane stood at the door and smiled at Doctor Hedtolg. "Thank you Doctor, but I think I'm going to be OK" he said, raising his hand to gesture goodbye as he left Dr Hedtolg for the last time.

Later that evening, Kane lay in a restless slumber. Despite being asleep his constant fidgeting suggested otherwise beneath those veiled eyes.

Suddenly as if vacating a bad dream, he was woken and again by the same noises as before. Whatever had been bothering him in his sleep was secondary to what was currently bothering him in his awoken state.

Over the course of the past few weeks, Kane had lay still, in a state of fear and panic, every time his room had been taken over by this strange noise. Tonight though was to be his last night in the room and he decided, enough was enough. Doctor Hedtolg was right, it almost certainly was a figment of his imagination and he figured that if he ignored it and took no notice, the sound would eventually be swallowed into the darkness and his brain would tire of harassing him.

"Faah Paah" the noise continued, every so often.

Kane tried his hardest to ignore it but the sound gradually broke him down and got the better of him. Whatever he wanted to believe, he knew there was no denying it, the sound was there, in the room.

He slowly and quietly sat up in bed as the whispering sound continued in the room and switched on the light above his bed.

He froze with fear and almost screamed out. Expecting to see nothing but his empty room, he was caught unaware by what appeared before him.

There in the darkened corner of the lamp lit room, sat a little girl, only around six or seven years old, tightly holding a small brown toy bear. Kane noticed, before anything else, that the bear was missing an eye and in its place were strands of cotton and fluff. The girl was looking straight at him and chattering away constantly, but Kane could not hear a thing, apart from the occasional "faaah Paaah" which appeared to be audible every time she said whatever it was.

He sat frozen in bed, staring at the grey features of this spectre standing there before him. Watching her for what felt like ages, He was rather relieved that he was not, in fact, going mad, the sound maker existed.

Suddenly the ashen faced girl got up and walked over to him, quickly, too quickly and all of a sudden she was standing directly in front of him, her face close to his.

"What do you want?" he asked her, trying to keep calm. "What do you want, I want to help you." he said.

All of a sudden the girl stopped her silent talking and looked at him intently. She could see Kane as clearly as he could see her. It felt as though she was staring deep into his soul. The child's eyes were sad and thoughtful. She appeared to have a lifetime of stories in them. For what seemed like an age, Kane sat motionless while the ghostly child stood opposite him. She was close enough to be practically nose to nose and he could feel the wintry chill of her breath blowing over his face.

Slowly, she opened her mouth and finally said two words, crystal clear and practically digital in their audibility. Kane didn't register what she had said straight away and seeming to sense this, the child repeated them again, still staring into Kane's pupils.

"Finnigan's Point." she said, never once diverting her gaze away from him.

"Finnigan's Point?" replied Kane in a dry throated whisper.

As if his acknowledgement of what she had said was all that was required from him, she disappeared, literally, right in front of his eyes. He sat there, motionless still, his brain struggling to register exactly what it was he had just witnessed. As if overcome with exhaustion from the whole experience, he passed out, fortunately still in the soft cushioning grasp of the bed.

The following morning a young Scottish Doctor named McCewan came in the room. Kane had spoken to him a few times since he'd been in the hospital and had always liked him.

"Last day I understand Mr Kane" said the Doctor, "Sleep well for once last night?"

"Not bad" he lied, "The usual strange dreams and noises, but nothing to write home about."

"So you're still getting noises eh Mr Kane that's a wee bit odd now isn't it?" said Dr McCewan as he ticked a couple of boxes on the chart housed at the end of his bed.

"Ever heard of Finnigan's Point?" asked Kane. Dr McCewan looked at him with a puzzled expression.

"Yes, of course, it's in the outer Hebrides" he replied. "Never been there myself, heard it's nice though, why?"

Kane looked surprised the place actually existed and was even more surprised by what next came out of his mouth. "I'm thinking of going there." he said.

Chapter Seven

As Doctor Hedtolg had promised, Kane was released that very day, following the confirmation of his clean bill of health. He had been careful not to tell anybody about the ghostly girl he'd seen in his room, mainly because he wasn't sure if it was real, a dream, or his subconscious. Whatever the answer, he had no intention of staying in that hospital any longer, he felt he had done his time and earned his release.

That "Finnigan's Point had in fact been a real place was quite surprising to him. Before the previous evening he had never heard of the place before. He had no idea what it was, but figured that it sounded as though it was a place, rather than an object or person.

The following day he spent his time in the library, somewhere he'd rarely been since a child. Walking into the silent and dusty library brought back cheerful memories. Kane had enjoyed visiting the library as a child and had always been an avid reader. The fact there was a place which existed whereby he could borrow books for free had always fascinated him. Nowadays nothing came for free, but as ever, the trusty library still did. The main change that he could see was the replacement of the old manual system with an electronic one. That though, was par for the course, mostly everywhere nowadays and was no surprise to him. The other major change of course had been the advent of the Internet, something the library also allowed free access to. The Worldwide Web had been a useful tool as a Detective, private and public and he spent some time looking up Finnigan's Point, trying to find out as much as he could. The Doctor had been correct, it was up in the Hebrides and in facts sounded very nice and quaint. The perfect picturesque village so to speak. The information on the internet was fairly sketchy, limiting itself to mainly directions on how to get there, scattered between the occasional photograph.

Kane decided he must have heard of it some place before and the 'apparition' really had been his own mind. In the cold light of day, he couldn't really believe what he had seen had been real. It all seemed totally unfeasible now. He decided, if anything, the voice had been his subconscious, telling him it was time for a break. He agreed with his inner self, it was time.

Of course, he'd had recuperation time in the Hospital, but that was not quality time, or chosen time, that situation had been forced upon him. What he really needed was a real break away, a real holiday. Looking at Finnigan's Point on line had confirmed, if nothing else, that it was a far cry from the dank, dour crime ridden sludge hold of a place he was currently residing in.

The one good thing about not having any friends, family or indeed a life, was that he spent the majority of his time working and therefore little to no time at all doing anything remotely associated with socialising or relaxation. Consequently he had a sizeable amount of savings, this was the particular rainy day he'd decided he must have been saving for. Once again, the heavens were opened up and the dark and moody sky flooded its tears down on an unforgiving world below.

As he packed for his trip, he didn't care, he was just glad to be going away. The change of scenery would, he was sure, do him some good.

The following morning, after a heavy sleep, he awoke early, just as he usually did, only this time, to do something for himself. This he was not used to. It was unchartered territory.

With his small case and a marginally small change of clothes, Kane ran down to his reliable, but unfashionable, brown Ford Cortina. He loved the car, because it loved him, he could tell. Wherever he was willing to go, he'd bet his life that car was willing to go there too. It had never let him down and he'd had it twelve years. To own a car for as long as that and never once have to get dirty was fantastic and to own a car as old as that with the same outcome, an absolute miracle. He appreciated the old car more than anything else he owned. It was his most priceless possession.

He knew the journey was long and already decided he'd be better off stopping for the night, hopefully around half way there, if not further. As the rain continued to fall, he set off on his journey, expecting the bad weather to be a hindrance.

For as long as he had been able to, he'd always found it difficult to drive without music. For him the two went hand in hand and he could not envisage doing one without the other.

Strangely, he rarely listened to music at home, mainly because he didn't own any. As he set off, he switched the radio on, he was met with the usual hissing you get when it's not tuned in properly.

The radio in the car was much the same as the car itself, old and outdated. An analogue dial, something that nowadays was becoming a thing of the past, along with cassette and vinyl.

He switched the dial from left to right and was met by the same hissing tone throughout. He then moved from FM to medium wave and was met with the same response. To pick up no stations at all was strange but he also thought if the radio was the only thing to go wrong on this car throughout the whole journey, then he could easily live with that.

The daylight began to creep through the heavy clouds above, however not so much that anybody would notice it. The heavy gloom above had made it practically impossible for some weeks now to tell when night turned to day and vice versa.

Half an hour into the journey he arrived at a petrol station and decided it best to fill up to the max, therefore reducing his amount of stopping times. He pulled up and got out of his car. The lights were on in the foyer but that aside, it looked as though the whole place was closed. He put the pump in the car and pressed the nozzle. Petrol flowed and that fantastic, yet dangerous smell, rose up from the nozzle. He'd yet to meet anyone not seduced by the smell of petrol. It was a fantastic aroma, his favourite.

As he ventured into the petrol station he was met by the gaze of the attendant, clearly disinterested in being there. "You a taxi driver?" he asked Kane, staring out of the window at a vehicle obviously not a taxi.

"No, I'm not, I'm going away for a bit." he replied.

"Where to?" asked the attendant. Kane could have said the moon and the attendant would have been no more interested. "Place up North, called Finnigan's Point" he responded, not wanting to. It had nothing to do with the attendant. Kane wasn't particularly sociable when people he didn't know spoke to him. He'd always been the same.

"Never heard of it" said the attendant. He wasn't surprised by this, until the day before yesterday neither had he. He picked up a cassette from the counter and slid it forward to pay for it. The attendant looked at it. "You like Stevie Wonder?" he asked. As he passed the money over, he looked at the attendant with a cutting glare.

"No, no I hate him." he responded sarcastically, before taking his change and walking out.

Kane had given up on morons a long time ago, the country was full of them. He could never understand why people would refuse to educate themselves in any way and then ask him questions like he was the stupid one. He climbed back into the car and put the cassette in the radio's slot. He had no idea if the cassette player even worked. He couldn't think of one occasion when he'd ever used it.

"For Once in My Life" blared out of the speakers and he quickly turned the volume down. Yes, the cassette player definitely worked, but he didn't want to drive along sounding like a boy racer. He then wondered just how many boy racers thundered along in their souped-up gleaming machines with Stevie Wonder blaring out and decided that probably none ever had.

For the next few hours he travelled as most people do. He encountered the obligatory traffic jam, the essential road rage incident and the compulsory accident, with guaranteed bottle necking, just to slow him down further. He stopped at one of the numerous roadside chefs he passed and was greeted by the same miserable people who worked in all of them, as if they were always one step ahead of him down the motorway. After treating himself to some badly cooked, over priced food, eaten with cutlery still caked in the last persons dinner and washed away with watered down coke, He set off once again.

39

He'd enjoyed the leg stretch, even if the lunch was almost certainly going to leave him in need of the toilet when he couldn't find one, or puking later on in the afternoon. Either way, he knew he'd end up regretting the stop.

As the gloomy day became gloomier, signalling another nightfall, he came across an off road motel. As he pulled up it looked like the Norman Bates variety but he decided that beggars can't be choosers and as long as he didn't take a shower, he'd probably be ok. He walked into reception where a young man not at all dissimilar to Norman Bates, greeted him. He paid for his room and made his way over for what he hoped would be a good nights sleep, ahead of the final part of his journey the following day.

Opening the door, he walked into the room and turned on the light. He wasn't sure what he'd expected to find, but he was amused at the thought of everyone he knew standing there and yelling surprise! as the light flicked into life. Kane's amusement quickly subsided when he realised that everyone he knew would fit inside a phone box, with room to spare.

He looked around at the generic motel room, throwing his bag down before slumping on to the bed. He was asleep in seconds. driving was surprisingly shattering.

Chapter Eight

The three boys cautiously peered into the bag together. None of them were prepared to admit what was in there, even Terrence, the orchestrator of the surprise.

"A gun?" Harvey finally said, "Where the bloody hell did you get a gun?!"

Terrence looked solemn. "It was my Dads. I saw it once a few years ago, he put it in a box up in the loft. He thought I hadn't seen it but I had. I only remembered it in the week" he said.

"Your Mum will go ape shit." Chris said, with a hint of a smile in his eyes.

"She doesn't even know it exists," Terrence said, "She hasn't a clue."

"Why'd your Dad have a gun?" Harvey asked, "People don't really have guns in this country."

He was right as well, Britain wasn't over run with guns, far from it in fact. That was something best left to the Americans, so why had Terrence's Dad had a gun?

"No idea," he admitted, "I haven't really asked myself that question before. I always thought it would turn out to be a pretend one, but it's definitely real."

"Perhaps he was a murderer?" Harvey said, without thinking. Chris smacked him round the back of the head.

"Perhaps you're a bloody idiot." Chris said to him. "So Terrence, what are we going to do with this then?"

Terrence hadn't really thought that far ahead, he just knew the guys would think it was super cool if he brought the gun out with him, he could tell he was right. What to do with it though? Now for the bad news, he decided.

"There's only 6 bullets," he said. "I couldn't find any more, perhaps there aren't any? " The excitement on Chris and Harvey's faces rapidly diminished.

"That's only three goes each" said Harvey.

Chris and Terrence looked at him. "That is why you're in the bottom class for maths." Chris said, "We can shoot cans or something, they'll be all sorts of things in the woods to shoot at." he continued.

Terrence was slightly regretting bringing the gun out now. With his Dad gone, he felt kind of safe knowing that gun was up there to protect both he and his Mum. If he used all of the bullets today, then it would never be up there to use again. Not only that, it would be another part of his Dad gone forever and Terrence didn't think there were many parts left as it was. He didn't tell the others that the only reason he really ever went in the loft was because it was the last place which really reminded him of his Dad, it had his smell. Either that or his Dad always smelt of the loft. Either way, he was that much closer to him just being in that damp and dark old loft. The three boys climbed over the fence that separated them from the woodland and with the gun safely tucked away in the bag, Terrence secretly hoped the others would just forget about it. On they walked, relieved of the shelter from the hot sun by the trees. The smell of the woods was different to anything they encountered on their journey, nature had a fresh, unblemished scent about it. Every tree, with its own smell, amalgamated into one uplifting odour. The woods smelt, among other things, of life.

"What are we going to do today anyway?" Harvey asked, "I mean, now we're actually here." It was a fair question. They'd all decided to hike up to the woods as it was a nice day without really knowing exactly why they were going up there for in the first place. For practically the whole of the summer holiday so far they had done little to write home about. Playing on their bikes, playing football, at each others houses and generally, doing the usual things that boys always seemed to do.

"Well if we've come all this way it seems silly not to build a tree house," Chris said. They all agreed that was a good idea. They were surrounded with fallen trees, branches and all manner of things to build the perfect tree house with. "We should definitely build the tree house, but before we do, there's something here we need to see." Terrence said. Chris and Harvey both stopped to listen.

"What could there be to do that's more important than building the worlds coolest tree house?" Harvey said. "There's a haunted house here". Terrence replied with a serious, edgy tone to his voice. Chris started laughing at just about the same moment Harvey started wailing like a trapped animal.

"Are you having a laugh?" Chris asked. "A haunted house, there's no such things as haunted houses, ghosts and goblins, it's all made up" "Not true" said Harvey, "I've seen some really strange things before. There was this one night, I'm not joking either guys, this is deadly serious ......"

Both Terrence and Chris interrupted him with their sniggers. It wasn't as if they didn't believe Harvey had something important to tell them, it was the look of intensity on his face. He looked like a twelve year old destined for as stroke.

"I'm not telling the story if you're going to take the mickey out of me," Harvey said, "Forget it."

"No, no, tell the story, we won't take the pee, I promise." Chris lied. Harvey geared himself up for the story. Both the boys could tell this was going to be one hell of a tale. Harvey loved making things up so much the two of them really didn't know when he was telling the truth or not. He'd gained a reputation at school for his off the wall ramblings. Sometimes, and not often, Harvey would tell the truth, but his reputation for weaving the most unbelievable of tales always proceeded him. In fact Harvey had found himself on the wrong end of the Teachers wrath on more than one occasion, even when he was actually telling the truth.

"OK there was this one time," Harvey began, "I heard this noise in the night, I don't know what it was, but it was like a moaning, a long wailing moaning noise, that got louder and louder"

"What, and you were in bed?" Terrence asked.

"Yes it was late, I was trying to sleep. Anyway I hear this moaning and wailing noise and then this banging noise and I'm hiding under the covers. I'm not joking either, I thought I was going to wet the bed, it was terrifying!" Terrence and Chris burst out laughing at this, but Harvey didn't care.

"Yeah, that may sound funny, but I was desperate for the loo and I couldn't get up because of this awful noise, so I had to hold it." he said "So what did you do?" Chris asked, still sniggering. "I waited for as long as possible and the noise died down. Then I heard my Mum and Dad talking so I thought they must have been woken up by it as well." Chris laughed at this.

"You dimwit, it was your Mum and Dad making the noise, you're such a fool." He said. Harvey looked puzzled as Terrence realised the source behind the strange noises. "Why would my Mum and Dad make noises just to scare me?" Harvey asked. The two boys laughed out loud at that. "Your Mum and Dad were, you know, doing things in the bed room, like we learned about at school." Terrence said.

Harvey went a little red and looked angry at the two of them.

"Yeah" he said, in defiance, "Well then explain how I saw a frightening and scary face in the bathroom mirror when I did eventually get up for the toilet?" he asked them.

"That was your reflection." said Chris, as he and Terrence laughed again.

"You two always make fun of me," said Harvey, "I knew you would".

"Sorry Harv" said Terrence, "We just can't help it, there's so much to make fun of." The boys all had a laugh at this, including Harvey. After they'd all calmed down they realised they had walked so far, they were now at the top of a dirt track which led down a long and steep hill, into a darker, denser area of the woods.

"It's down there," said Terrence, pointing down the track. The three boys looked down into the dark wooded cavern.

"What is?" whispered Chris, himself sounding less assured now.

"The haunted house," replied Terrence. "In fact, its not a haunted house, it's where a witch used to live."

No one said anything and none of them was prepared to make fun of this. Terrence didn't make things up and both the boys could see he was being deadly serious.

"How'd you know all this crap?" Harvey asked him.

"My Dad told me about it when we first came here, he told me not to go down there." Terrence said.

"He was just having a laugh", Chris replied, still whispering. "Wasn't he?"

The three boys stood at the top of the wooded path for what seemed like an eternity. None of them were prepared to go back, but each of them secretly hoped one of the others would crack first. After a couple of minutes of just standing and staring, Chris finally spoke.

"Lets do it, let's go down there and find this so called witches house." The three of them remained rooted to the spot, their legs weighed down with the adrenaline coursing through them. They could barely move.

"OK, let's go." said Terrence and began to lead the way. The three boys walked, slowly, none of them speaking, down the leaf covered path. All three of them seemed to be tuned into the surrounding area, with every little noise previously unnoticed making each of them jump ever so slightly.

Eventually they arrived at the bottom of the pathway, where the heavy overgrowth made it so much darker. Sure as the day was long, an old white house sat just off the path. It was practically derelict and clearly hadn't been lived in for many years, if ever. The three boys stared at it in wonder.

"It's just an old house," Harvey said, "What's scary about that?"

The three boys made their way towards the building and then through a hole where a wall would have once been. There was nothing of interest there at all. The leaves from the trees carpeted the area that would have been the floors. Essentially they were standing amongst a group of concrete blocks.

"My toilet's are more haunted than this." Chris said, they all laughed. Suddenly, the laughter stopped, as a crack echoed through the woodlands. "Did you hear that?" Harvey asked. All three of them looked around, again, the sounds of a twig cracking could be heard, as if stepped on by an invisible pair of feet. Subconsciously the three of them made their way out of the rubble and back onto the path, slowly making their way up the hill. Climbing up was going to be nowhere near as easy as coming down, but none of them had thought about that on the initial journey.

Suddenly the bushes started moving, as if somebody was behind them. All three boys heard the rustling and spied what appeared to be some movement and simultaneously, they ran, as fast their little legs would allow them to, in an almost perfect one hundred and eighty degree angle. As they neared the top of the hill, Terrence looked back. He screamed at the sight of what he was sure was a woman, standing at the bottom of the hill. The sound of his scream spurred both him and the boys on, picking up record speeds as they ran through the woodland, all screaming at the tops of their voices.

Finally, they got to an area where the sunlight clawed its way through the trees again and the threatening woodlands turned back into a picturesque Disney cartoon.

"What the hell did you scream for?" Chris asked. All of a sudden Harvey stepped back a little and disappeared into the ground, screaming. Terrence and Chris stood there, looking at a hole in the ground where their friend had previously been standing.

Chapter Nine

Kane woke up, covered in beads of sweat. It was not the first time he'd recently dreamt of his past childhood, but it was the first time he'd ever dreamt anything in sequence like that. He remembered the dream from start to finish and he knew it was perfectly re-enacted in his head. It was as if he had revisited that day all over again. There was one thing he was sure of, he'd like the dreaming in sequence to stop right there, it wasn't normal. Ever since he'd been shot he hadn't felt the same, as if something inside had died. Still, he was grateful for one thing and that was the cessation of the whispering voice when he had finally left the hospital.

Looking at his watch he saw it was already half past six which for him was a lie in. He wanted to get on the road as soon as possible so had a quick shower. The showers in those roadside hotels were invariably useless anyway, so there was never a desire to stay in them for too long, but this one was like a full on power wash. The shower was so violently strong, he thought himself lucky that he'd not switched it on over his face. If he had, he'd be blind and skinless by now.

Once dressed and with his few belongings packed, he went down and threw his bag into the car. Again, the sky looked full of rain. How could there be that much up there, he wondered, it was as if someone had turned the tap on above and left it, the recent downfall had been so relentless.

As he shut the boot of the car he was distracted by a voice calling him from behind. "Mr Kane, Mr Kane!"

He looked up and saw the motel owner in the doorway beckoning him over. 'This is where he throws his Mums dress on and chops me up' he thought as he strolled over to the man.

"How can I help you?" he asked.

The Motel manager pointed back inside to the reception. "You paid for the night, that includes breakfast" he said.

He was never one to label people, but the motel manager had the archetypal inbred look about him. Kane was sure his Mother was his cousin as well as his Sister.

"I'm not worried about breakfast" he said. "I don't eat it usually. I find it starts my metabolism off early and then I tend to get hungrier earlier".

The manager just looked at him. "I don't know what that is," he said, with Kane assuming he meant metabolism. "You've paid for your breakfast, you may as well have it, you have a long drive as well." he said.

He thought for a moment. "How'd you know I have a long drive?" he asked him.

"Stands to reason," the man said, "You didn't stop here because you were five minutes from home.

He decided the man made sense, perhaps for the first time.

"OK, if I've paid for it, I may as well have it."

He followed the man into the Motel. There was literally nobody else in sight. It seemed as though both he and the Motel Manager were the only two people there. He figured that in a place that small, that may just be the case.

"If I'm going to have it, I may as well have the full English Breakfast." He said as the Manager seated him in the world's smallest restaurant. There were two tables, both in the reception area still and he was now seated at one of them. This was first class if ever he had seen it. Fortunately, he hadn't, so he had no expectations to live up to.

"I don't know what that is" the Manager said again, "We have a choice of cereals and jams." he continued.

Kane didn't know what to say next, spoilt for choice as he was. "Which cereals do you have?" he politely asked.

The manager thought for a minute. "Corn Flakes." he said finally.

He waited for something to be added to the list. "You said there was a choice?" he remarked.

"There is, said the Manager, "You have Corn Flakes or no Corn Flakes".

48

He hated corn flakes, always had ever since he was a kid. If you didn't eat it within five seconds it became as wet and soggy as rain soaked toilet paper and about as tasty too.

"No, don't worry about it, which jams have you got?" he asked. The manager was now looking fed up with him, seeming to forget that he was the reason Kane was sitting there in the first place.

"Just strawberry." he said. He didn't mind strawberry and at least he could end this farce and get himself back on the road soon.

"Jam on toast then it is, my man." he said, trying to humour his host. The Manager looked at him.

"We don't have any bread." he said.

Kane's patience was beginning to stretch. "What the bloody hell am I meant to eat the jam with then?" he asked, in an agitated manner.

"A spoon." said the Manager, looking at him like he was the one missing a few brain cells. "What else would you eat jam with?".

"So basically I get a jar of jam for breakfast? well that sounds just yummy," he said as sarcastically as he could. "Fetch me that jar and a spoon as soon as possible, I'm famished." he continued. He could tell the Manager was not familiar with sarcasm, as he quickly scampered off to get the breakfast treat.

When he returned, Kane had already got in the car and driven away unable to witness the miniature jam and dessert spoon, too big for the jars opening, that had been brought back.

With Stevie Wonder's 'My Cherie Amour' blaring away in the car, he was feeling quite happy. He didn't think he had too far to go now and although the rain had indeed began to rattle off the cars bonnet again like a harmless machine gun, he didn't care. He was enjoying the open road.

All of a sudden a loud 'thunk' rapidly changed his whole opinion. 'thunk, thunk, thunk.'

He knew instantly, just by the pull of the steering wheel, that he'd gained a puncture. Now the pleasant and inviting raindrops sounded menacing and intrusive. He was about to get soaked through. Ordinarily he would have waited for the rain to subside, but the way things had been going recently, he couldn't be bothered to sit on the hard shoulder for six weeks.

He pulled in where it was safe, not that there were a great amount of cars around and climbed out of the car to survey the damage. The rain was more torrential and relentless than it looked inside the vehicle, but he had little option but to roll with it. He was reminded of his favourite programme as a child, The Incredible Hulk, and how he first turned into the green beast while changing a tyre in the pouring rain. Kane would do anything to turn into a hulking giant of a man right now, but as that was never going to happen, he'd just have to settle for getting soaked and mildly annoyed.

After ten minutes of fighting the weather, the slip of the tyre iron from his wet hands and the locked nuts on the wheel, he was finally done. He hated not having a spare tyre and figured he'd have to get one as soon as he got to Finnigan's Point, if he could. Leaving the old tyre by the side of the road, he got back in the car, soaked to the bone.

'I should get to Finnigan's Point just in time to catch my cold' he thought to himself.

He continued on his journey, stopping only once to use the toilet at a roadside stopping point. The weather brightened up and the sun came out just as he approached a faded road sign, pointing down a beaten looking dirt track. 'Finnigan's Point this way' it said, in large letters. Had it still been raining, he was pretty sure he would have completely missed the turn off. He followed the muddy track for only a couple of miles, seeming to drive the whole distance right through the middle of a field. The car was lined on either side with recently harvested corn fields as far as the eye could see. Suddenly, as if they popped up out of the landscape from nowhere, a row of around three houses appeared in the distance. At the end of the dirt track and the beginning of a road sat a large sign, brightly painted in greens, reds and blues. "Welcome to Finnigan's Point." it screamed out of it's wooden backdrop and Kane instantly felt right at home.

Chapter Ten

As he drove through the town, he marvelled at it's unparalleled beauty. He really had never seen anything like it, at least not in the flesh. The whole area had a fantastical technicolour surrounding. The grass was vividly green, the sky cartoonish blue, the water as clear as crystal and the air as clear as the day the earth was created. Having not ventured out of his dank and dismal town for the majority of his adult life, this place was always gong to have an impact on him.

On either side of the narrow road was cast untouched greenery, intermingled with the occasional small home. A lake to his right, with ducks freely swimming and picturesque woodland up ahead of him. What he though were a row of houses when he arrived were in fact a grocers, a general store and a post office. The whole place was as quaint and eye catching as he had hoped and he knew he would get the chance to recuperate properly here, without any problems at all. In its silent calm, Finnigan's Point screamed solitude at him.

As he continued to drive, the occasional onlooker paid him a distant glance without ever really looking at who was arriving. He could tell the people were all wondering exactly who the newcomer to their town may be, at least he felt they should be. For all he knew, these onlookers may be dead set against outsiders in Finnigan's Point and could easily turn him away and back home as soon as he debarked from his car. This could be the archetypal local town for local people.

Up on his left, he saw a beautiful wood surrounded hotel. Almost log cabin in its appearance, but clearly three stories high.

The vacancy sign was displayed neatly in the downstairs window and he knew he had to grab the room before anybody else arrived and snatched it from his grasp. He had been lucky, until now it hadn't occurred to him to book ahead.

51

Parking his car in one of the few spaces outside he got out of the car, stretched his legs and entered the hotel. There were few feelings better than the one which came with standing up following a long drive.

The reception was manned by an elderly lady, grey hair, wrinkled face and withered in her appearance. Her eyes lit up and shone a twinkle as her gaze fell upon him. In an instant she'd gone from looking seventy to seventeen and greeted him with a huge smile.

"Ooh lovely" she said, "A newbie. There's few things more interesting than the arrival of a new guest. Welcome to Finnigan's Inn". "Thank you very much" he held out his hand which she took within her wrinkled arthritic grasp and graciously shook.

"Terrence Kane." he said, in introduction. The old lady continued to smile.

"I'm Gretna Greene, very pleased to meet you."

Kane started laughing. "Gretna Greene! Very good, really, what is your name?"

The old lady laughed. "My parents idea of a joke I guess, but it really is Gretna Greene".

He stopped laughing, he could tell she was being serious.

"I apologise," he said sheepishly. "I didn't mean to be rude".

"No worries at all," Gretna replied. "It's not the first time I've had that response and I doubt it will be the last. How long are you wishing to stay for?". She asked, neatly changing the subject. He pondered for a moment. He hadn't really put a great deal of thought into how long he was going away for, but with no commitments or responsibilities waiting for him back home, there was no urgency for him to return.

"Can I make it open ended?". he asked, hopefully. Gretna checked the book on the desk in front of her, flicking through the pages.

"No problem at all," she responded. "Stay as long as you like. I have no bookings, or reservations for, well, forever, so I guess you'll be OK to stick around for one day or one year, whatever you wish." she finished.

"I doubt I'll stick around for a year, but you never know, so put me down for a "will leave one day". He said.

"Well everybody always does in the end I'm afraid." said Gretna.

"Out of interest," he said, "Why is it you have no advance bookings, I mean a place like this, as picturesque and tranquil, should be fully booked all year long." Gretna just smiled.

"Rarely does anybody book in advance," she said. "In fact, we get most of our business from people just turning up and passing through, just like yourself!" He supposed that was fair enough, it was the kind of idyllic place you could just come across and given that the directions to the beaten track were so easily obscured, he doubted they got many visitors around here.

"How much will it be"? he asked, fishing around in his pocket for some cash. "It's £10 per night." Gretna replied. He quickly glanced at her to gauge whether she was joking or not and could see, she probably wasn't. "Ten pounds!" he exclaimed. "Are you sure?" Gretna started to look a little worried.

"Is that too much?", she asked, nervously. "Because that does include breakfast".

"Too much?" he laughed, "Not at all, it's beyond reasonable, how do you make a profit charging so little?"

"We do OK here," Gretna said. "My husband and I have been running this place for as long as we can remember and its still here, so we must be doing something right I guess". Kane couldn't disagree with that, but still, they could make a killing if they charged the right prices.

"I'd like to meet your husband at some point," he replied. "He sounds like a very reasonable man."

"Oh he is Mr Kane, everybody thinks so, I'm sure you will meet John eventually, everybody knows him".

He paid for his room, giving Gretna seventy pounds for the whole week. Even though she'd insisted that was the price, he couldn't help but feel like he had fleeced her in some way. While Gretna fished around in the till, he thought of something else he wanted to ask her, before he went to his room.

"Is there anything to do here other than relax, which is what I intend to do anyway?" he asked.

"There's a bar just behind this place, if you go there you'll meet mostly everyone, its the one place they can get together and have a good time" she said. "That's great, what more could I ask

for, beer and relaxation! I must have died and gone to heaven."
he said, Gretna laughed.

"God probably doesn't allow beer in Heaven, although I
guess in a way, he invented it, or at least the ingredients, so
perhaps he does," She reached over to the wall behind her and
grabbed a key marked with a number four. "Just up the stairs and
to the right," she said, "I hope you enjoy your stay Mr Kane."

"I fully intend to." he replied, grinning.

He made his way up the wooden stairs to his room. The
building smelt old, but in a nice way. It had a lot of character and
he liked that, it was homey, without being home.

He opened the big heavy wooden door to his room and looked
in. Glancing around he noted how surprisingly spacious the
room looked. The bed was big and like the building itself, the
room had a strong emphasis on the wooden surroundings with
the bed clothes and various furniture fittings being brown
coloured or wooden in appearance. He loved it straight away.
Quickly looking in the bathroom he saw an old fashioned shower
in the bath, running from the taps instead of a unit on the wall.
The bathroom was clean at least. He had a little shiver as he
remembered the bathroom in the motel he had stayed in only the
night before, with its mouldy tiles and filth covered bath. Kane
had mused there were so many rings around that bath he could
have estimated how old it was. Now he had arrived at Finnigan's
Point, the night before already seemed like a distant memory.

Looking around again he realised there was something
missing. It hadn't been obvious at first, until he'd looked for it,
but there was no TV. With some people, this would be a cause
for alarm and panic, but not for him. He had never been one for
the television, he rarely saw anything that didn't make him feel
angry or upset nowadays, for him no TV meant no stories about
rape, murder, famine and war and that was in no way a bad thing.
Even the programmes designed to entertain these days seemed
destined to upset and disturb. He knew he could definitely get
used to this place. He also knew, that with his few belongings
neatly stowed away, he should make his way round the grocery
store and buy a few things for his stay. Unnoticed he slipped out
of the hotel. Gretna Greene was nowhere in sight.

Making his way up the short road, the sun still beaming down, he quickly came to the grocery store. Walking in, he saw the usual supplies you would expect to find, bread, milk, toothpaste etc. He also saw the young woman behind the counter, briefly eyeing him up and down. With a small basket filled with various things, he made his way over to pay. The woman serving was fairly short with dark brown hair and a slim physique. Kane hadn't really had an eye for the ladies for some while, he never had the time, but this woman had certainly caught his eye in an instant. "Terrence Kane." he announced, introducing himself, although nobody had asked, while placing his basket down on the counter. The woman merely looked at him as she keyed the prices of his goods into the till.

"How long are you intending to stay here Mr Kane?" she asked him.

"For as long as I need to really," he replied, "and please, call me Terrence". The woman didn't smile, in fact, she didn't do much at all. "That will be three pounds and fifteen pence please Mr Kane." the woman said. He looked at the items he had just bought and not for the first time that day decided he'd been under charged.

"No that doesn't seem enough," he said. The woman just looked at him and put her hand out. "It's what I said it was," she replied, looking slightly exasperated. "I know the prices of my own products."

Kane put his hand in his pocket and paid her the money. As he left the shop he glanced back, to see her looking at him again. "Never judge a book by its cover." he thought to himself. He still liked the woman though, with her hazel eyes and full lips, she was positively stunning. He knew he'd have enough time to find out more about her, perhaps even her name! She certainly hadn't appeared too eager to speak to him anyway.

With his shopping bag swinging randomly this way and that, from his hand, he made his way down to the lake. There sat a rather large man, with jeans and a t-shirt on, quietly fishing away, he had never been fishing, but instinctively knew fishermen do not like to be disturbed. As he turned to leave, the man spoke out in a deep rough voice. "Hey there", he said "Where are you going?" Kane stopped and turned back. "Just back to the hotel." he replied. The man was still looking at the lake, but turned when he spoke. All along the man had been talking to the fish he just let go, not Kane. "Hi, Paul Ryan." he said, holding out his hand to shake. He made his way over and grabbed Paul's hand. He had a big manly handshake, practically breaking the bones in Kane's fingers. "Terrence Kane," he replied. "I'm here on holiday." Paul laughed. "Ain't we all, fucking amazing place ain't it, absolutely beautiful. I love it here." he said. He nodded his head in agreement. "So you're here on holiday as well then?" he asked.

"Yep, been here three weeks already, marvellous place, I don't want to go." Paul replied.

"You staying much longer?" he asked. Paul nodded his head. "As long as I can get away with. You just got here?" he asked.

"Today, not long ago, staying in the hotel over there" he replied. pointing in the direction of the hotel. "That's great," Paul said, "So am I. Listen, if you're not doing anything later, then come over to the bar with me, I'll introduce you around. The people here are great, you'll enjoy it." He couldn't see any reason why not. It would be a good opportunity to get to know the people he'd be living alongside for the foreseeable future and if he was lucky, the woman from the shop may be there. "That would be great," he said. "I'll definitely do that, I will see you later then."

Paul shook Kane's hand again. "I'll give you a knock on my way out, what room are you in?" he asked. He told him his room number then said he'd see Paul later.

After a brief walk, he found himself back at the hotel. Once he got back to the room he had a quick look out of the window. The place was perfect and he'd received a fairly decent welcome. He was looking forward to meeting everybody else in the town later. For once in his life, he felt relaxed and stress free. He could tell, Finnigan's Point was going to be one of the best decisions he'd ever made.

56

Chapter Eleven

He walked the short distance with Paul round to the bar. The night air was cool but he wore no jacket, there was an air of comfort about the breeze. He hadn't seen any rain since he arrived in Finnigan's Point and considering the way the weather had been leading up to his journey, that was nothing short of a minor miracle. "You'll like the guys," Paul said. "They're a good bunch of nice ordinary people." Kane was quite looking forward to meeting new people. Usually for him meeting new people revolved around working with them in some capacity so this was going to make a welcome change for him. "That's great, hope I'm not intruding though." he said. Paul laughed. "Not at all, they're looking forward to meeting you." "You already told them about me then?" He asked, seeming surprised. "Absolutely!" Paul said.

He didn't speak again as they approached the bar. Kane wasn't bothered though, he hated it when people spoke for no reason other than to have something to say, even if it wasn't of any interest.

"Where do they live anyway?" He asked as they walked down the path that led to the bar. "In one of these houses?" he asked, gesturing around himself.

"No, not at all, they're on holiday, like us, staying in the motel." Paul said. Kane hadn't realised, he thought he was going to meet local people. It hadn't occurred to him there would be more holiday makers in town. He felt naive, Finnigan's Point was that sort of place after all.

The two men walked into the bar and unlike how you see it in the movies, nobody stopped what they were doing to look at them, everybody just carried on as normal, oblivious. There were a few people at the bar, two guys sitting at a table, a few more people over in the corner and on her own, the woman from the grocery store. The jukebox was playing 'Boys of Summer' by Don Henley, but not so loud you couldn't hear yourself think. One reason Kane had frequented bars and clubs on very few occasions, was the volume of noise in them. He couldn't understand how men went on to meet women in those places, it was impossible to speak or hear the other person.

Paul directed him over towards the table where the two other men sat and held the palm of his hand towards the men. "Guys this is Terrence Kane," he said. They each nodded their heads and then held out their hands to shake Kane's.

"Nice to meet you," they both said, almost simultaneously.

"This is Gerald Denson," Paul said, pointing towards a bearded man who looked as though he was in his late forties to early fifties, wearing thick rimmed glasses. "And this," Paul continued, "is Adam Peterson". This guy was younger, probably in his thirties, with short dark hair and a clean shaven face. Kane sat down while Paul headed off to the bar to get a round of drinks in, never asking anyone, including Kane, what they wanted to drink.

"Call me Gerry, not Gerald, nobody really calls me Gerald, well except my Mum and she's dead now, so nobody calls me Gerald." Kane smiled and just nodded his head. He wasn't going to tell anyone to call him Terry, he hadn't been called that since he was a kid. He quite liked being called Terrence anyway, it always made him feel slightly more respectable.

"So, what brings you here then Terrence?" Adam asked. "Nice place isn't it." he continued.

"Just fancied a break, you know, from the norm and yep, its a lovely place, I really like it here, unusually peaceful." he answered.

"It sure is peaceful," Gerald said. "What's so noisy about your life you needed to get away to the peace and quiet of Finnigan's Point?" he asked.

"Nothing really," he said. "I'm a Detective back home and I fancied an escape from that side of life, it can be pretty draining. What do you do?" he asked Gerald.

"I'm an accountant." he replied. Kane couldn't see any other job Gerald would suit, he screamed accountant every time he looked at him. He looked a Adam, trying to work out what his vocation would be. He guessed perhaps a mechanic, or some kind of manual labourer.

"And you, Adam, what's your job?" Kane asked him.

"I'm a writer." Adam said. Perfect place for him then, the tranquillity of Finnigan's Point could forge a book out of even the most reluctant of writers he figured.

"Nice place to write" Kane said. Adam nodded his head in agreement.

"Yeah it is, but I haven't written a word since I got here. Like you guys I came here to get away from what I do as well, even though this place is the most idyllic to do it in." Adam said.

Paul came back placed four beers on the table, before pulling out the only vacant chair and sitting down with everyone else.

"Terrence here was just telling us he's a detective." Adam said.

"Yeah?" Paul replied. "Perfect place to come and get away from that then eh! No detective work to do here." he continued, laughing.

"What do you do then?" He asked him. Paul looked slightly embarrassed. The other two laughed, knowing what he was going to say.

"Damn, I always hate answering this question," Paul said. "I'm an Estate Agent." he said, looking sheepish. Kane laughed at this.

"Nothing to be embarrassed about." he said.

"No, just ashamed." Adam said. They all laughed. Kane looked at the hands of all three men. None of them appeared to be married. Finnigan's Point seemed to attract the singleton.

"None of you guys married?" He asked.

"My wife died," Gerald said. "Car accident." Both Paul and Adam looked sorry for Gerald and Paul patted him on the back.

"Sorry." Kane said. Gerald looked as though he had briefly lost himself in his thoughts.

"No need to apologise." he finally responded.

"Anyway," said Paul, interrupting the awkwardness, "You are right, none of us are married. You?" he asked.

"No, never," Kane said. "Not met anyone I would want to spend the rest of my life with other than myself." he laughed.

The four of them sipped the beer for a few seconds, none of them saying anything.

"Who's the woman over there, the one from the shop?" Kane asked.

All three men looked round, straight at the woman, sitting there alone drinking a glass of wine.

"She's really rude, for no reason at all as well." Gerald said. Both Paul and Adam nodded their heads in agreement.

"Truth is none of us know her name," Adam said, "All we know is she's bloody rude, she will not speak to any of us."

"Think she has an aversion to the tourist kind." Paul said.

"Anyway, lets forget about the rude shopkeeper and get down to the real business," Adam said. Kane wasn't sure what was meant by Adam's statement.

"What business?" he asked, raising his eyebrows.

"Nothing, ignore him, he's an idiot." Paul said, looking at Adam.

"Ignore them both, what Adam is trying to say, and what I also want to know, is what do you have in common with us?" Gerald asked. He was puzzled, he had no idea what Gerald was going on about.

"How do you mean, in common with you?" Kane asked.

"What brought you here, how did you end up in Finnigan's Point?" Adam asked, as the others looked at Kane intensely, waiting for his answer.

"Nothing 'brought me here' as you put it, I just fancied a break, like I said, change of scenery," he replied. "Same as you guys." They all looked at each other.

"We were brought here," Paul said. "None of us chose to come here, we were made to come, directed here if you like". The others looked at Kane for a reaction. He was intrigued, the Detective in him wanted to know more.

"Explain what you mean?" He asked. All three men pulled their chairs in a bit further and leaned over the table.

"Voices," Adam said, "Did you have the voices?" The three men clearly had expected Kane to tell them he had, they waited like eager puppies anticipating their dinner.

"I'd never heard of this place before," Kane said, "I was told about it by... He stopped. "You know what," he continued.

"This is bullshit, I looked it up on the internet". The three men looked enormously disappointed. Paul looked at Kane suspiciously.

"So you came here of your own accord?" he asked. He didn't want to lie, but he wanted to find out more about their reasons for wanting to know first.

"Yeah, looked up breaks away on line and this place had a good reputation, so here I am." he replied.

"Strange." Adam said, as the other two guys nodded in agreement.

"So, how long have you guys been staying here then?" He asked them, quickly changing the subject.

"Four weeks." Adam said. "Three weeks." Gerald replied. "Six weeks." Paul answered. Kane was surprised, that was a long time for any holiday to last. He could tell neither one of them were really listening properly to him, their answers were disjointed and unfocused. What they wanted to know was why had he come here. He knew his internet story hadn't washed. All three men had gone from being relaxed and open with him to tenseness and caution.

"Bloody hell, six weeks, that's some holiday you're having there Paul," he said. "In fact, come to think of it, you're all having one hell of holiday. Any plans on leaving soon?" he asked everyone and nobody in particular. The three men looked at each other and then Paul leaned even further over the table until his nose was almost touching Kane's.

"We can't leave," he said. "We're stuck here." Kane laughed at the absurd comment. Nobody joined him.

"Yeah, that's your excuse," he smiled. "You can't leave here, more like you don't want to." he continued. Paul wore an expression of total seriousness on his face and Kane knew then he wasn't joking. Paul had gone from being fairly light and jovial to looking like the most unhappy man on the planet.

"There's no way out Terrence, we're trapped."

Kane stopped smiling.

"What are you three up to, the path is just round the corner, you follow it out to the dirt track and then onto the main road." All three men sat there with serious looks on their faces.

"We've all tried, individually and together," Gerald said. "That road just goes on forever, its never ending."

Kane looked at them all with a worried expression.

"Don't be ridiculous," he said. "If there's a way in, there's a way out, and that's the end of it. The way in doesn't suddenly disappear now does it?" he continued.

"We've been trying to get out for a couple of weeks now, it's gone, the exit has gone, we're trapped here." Adam said.

"That's totally fucking insane," Kane said. "All four of us are jumping in my car tomorrow and driving out of here. I guarantee you there's an exit onto the main road just a couple of miles up, otherwise how the hell did the four of us get here, by magic?"

"OK, we'll go with you tomorrow," Paul said, "If only to prove to you we're not going mad, we're trapped here and I'm willing to bet, so are you."

He laughed at them, but they were not laughing, all three of them wore masks of gloom.

Chapter Twelve

Kane awoke early and was surprised to find the three men waiting at his door when he opened it. All of them were eager to prove a point it appeared and he was equally as desperate to prove they had gone mad. Trotting downstairs and past Gretna Greene, who waved as they went out, the three men climbed into Kane's car.

"This is a total waste of time," Kane said, as they all got into the car. The other three said nothing. "You can't honestly expect me to believe this shit. I kind of hoped you'd made the whole thing up due to the alcohol, or something last night." he continued. None of them replied.

"Seriously guys, you want me to go through with this?" Seems a bit of an elaborate joke to me?" he continued.

"Reset your mileage counter," Adam said, "Then you'll see who's joking."

"I'm not resetting the mileage counter, I like to see how many miles I've driven when I get home, it interests me." Kane responded, indignantly.

"Just do it," Paul said. The jovial light hearted guys from the night before were now serious and heavy browed. Kane felt uncomfortable around them, they were all fairly intense. At first they'd seemed OK and he'd had a laugh with them last night, but really, did he know them? He was concerned about whether he could and should trust these men but, doing as he'd been asked, he reset the counter. At the very least he figured, it would merely help to prove his point. He knew he'd travelled along the road for a couple of miles before he'd reached Finnigan's Point so he had a pretty good idea this experiment wasn't going to last that long. His stomach grumbled, interrupting the current silence in the car. He was hungry for some breakfast, but figured he'd be back in twenty minutes, so his stomach would have to wait.

He started the engine and set off on the journey out of town. "Really guys," he said. "This does seem like a total waste of time, roads do not just disappear." No one said a thing, as the car left the quiet town of Finnigan's Point and manoeuvred along the same dusty road it came in on. As with the journey there, the fields lined either side of the path and there really was no other road and no alternative way you could accidentally go wrong. He was looking forward to laughing about all of this.

"Reminds me of that film," Gerald said, out of the blue.

"What, Deliverance?" Adam answered. They all laughed.

"Squeal Little Piggy." Paul said, unnervingly like an inbred yokel. Again they all laughed. Kane more nervously than anyone else. "Great," he thought to himself, I'm about to get gang raped!"

"Morons, I meant that Children of the Corn film." Gerald continued. "Outside of town is pretty bloody spooky."

"That's a shit film." Paul said, both Kane and Adam nodded.

"Stephen King books rarely get turned into good films." Kane said, pleased they were off the Deliverance comparisons.

"What about The Shining?" Paul said. Adam and Gerald agreed, but Kane did not.

"It's a good film, granted, but it's still not as good as the book. A film has got to be as good or better than the book to really set a benchmark." he said. "And there haven't been many films made from Stephen King books which have been as good as the book itself." Kane finished

"What about The Running Man?" Adam asked. Kane just laughed

"I'll tell you what," he said. "Name one different Stephen King book that has been turned into an equally good film." They all thought for a moment.

"Easy," said Gerald. "The Green Mile." They all nodded.

"Good choice, good choice," said Paul. "What about Stand by Me?" Kane and Gerald both nodded, while Adam started laughing.

"That's not a Stephen King story." Adam said, still laughing.

"It is, it was originally called "The Body" Kane said, Adam looked surprised.

"Seriously, I didn't know that, thought he only did scary." Adam replied. "No, he has a fantastic range and I'm going for The Shawshank Redemption, another non scary one." Kane said. Again everyone nodded their heads in agreement.

"Over to you then Adam, last one to think of one." Paul said. Adam sat there silent for a minute, trying to think of one. "What about Misery?" he said. None of them could agree. Kane liked it, but not as much as the book, Paul thought it should count as a good film and Gerald had never seen it.

"I know, I've got one," Adam said, enthusiastically bouncing in the car seat like a five year old.

"The Dead Zone!" he exclaimed. All of them agreed on that one.

"That's a great film." Kane said. Paul looked over at the dashboard.

"How many miles have you done Terrence?" he asked. Kane looked at the speedometer and then did a double take, looking again.

"Ten miles, that can't be right, that's impossible, already?" Nobody said anything as he looked ahead. All he could see was the dirt road he was already on and the fields, seemingly endless, on either side of him.

"That's impossible," he started tapping the speedometer. "This can't be right." he said again, looking over at Paul.

"Look in your rear view mirror." Gerald said. Kane did and was stunned at what he saw. There, just a couple of hundred yards back sat the entrance to Finnigan's Point. It appeared they hadn't gone anywhere, just been running on the spot.

Kane floored the accelerator and his speed hit over eighty. Still the view of Finnigan's Point became no smaller in the mirror. It was almost as if the four of them were being chased by the town. He stopped the car and turned off the engine.

"Now do you believe us?" Paul asked him. He nodded his head in disbelieving agreement.

"How is that even remotely possible?" he asked, knowing not one of them had the answer.

"It's not is it, logistically speaking," Gerald said, "And yet, here we are, we've all witnessed it, so explain it.?"

"Have you mentioned it to the people in town?" Kane asked.
"No one had, none of them wanted to appear clinically insane and that was probably a wise choice. Four of them had witnessed their failure to drive away from the town. Surely four people with the same story wouldn't be dismissed out of hand?

"When we asked you what you had in common with us, it was for a reason." Paul said.

"How do you mean?" He asked. "How can we have something in common when we don't even know each other?"

"We all came here for a reason," Adam said. "We were all drawn to this place out of the blue and within a few weeks of each other and we've all come here as well."

"You're the missing piece." Gerald said. Kane's look of bemusement increased further still.

"The missing piece?" he said, "To what, what the bloody hell does that mean?" He asked them.

It seemed they all had a story and one by one they relayed their tale of how they had been drawn to Finnigan's Point. It seemed that Gerald had heard the name whispered to him down the telephone before eventually he looked it up on the internet and found the place to be real and not some kind of figment of his imagination.

Paul had the same recurring dream every night for a month. He told them it involved him driving down this very road and entering the town, past the welcome sign Like Gerald he also had never heard of the place but when he found it was real he had to come and see how accurate his dreams were. Paul said he couldn't believe it when he arrived, it was almost as if he had become psychic out of the blue, even the tiniest detail was familiar to him.

Adam's story was the strangest by far. He had bought a newspaper as he did every day and while reading it found that a number of letters had been highlighted in fluorescent pen. Being a fan of puzzles Adam wrote all the letters down, expecting there to be some kind of cryptic message. All he got, over and over again, in sequence, was "Finnigan's Point". What interested them all about this story was how Adam's paper had been pre highlighted before he bought it. How could anyone know he was going to buy that one?

Kane relayed his story to them all, about the whispering and then the ghostly little girl, who whispered the name of the town to him. Everyone was of course intrigued.

"Why were you in hospital in the first place?" Paul asked. "What was wrong with you?"

Kane went on to then tell them the story about Donovan and the shooting. Again, they were all interested. He figured it was due to the fact it was a good story, but little did he know, there was another reason.

"What you have just said is very interesting." Gerald said.

"Why is it so interesting?" he asked.

"Because, Terrence" Gerald said.

"The four of us have even more in common than we think."

Chapter Thirteen

Gerald's Story

"Gerald, Gerald!" called the woman's voice in a shrill tone. Gerald had been married to Sally for over twenty years and still, after all of this time, she wasn't aware of just how much she nagged him, He'd told her often enough during one too many heated arguments, which couples invariably always have, but Sally had always elected to ignore those comments. Her incessant nagging of him about the slightest little thing had become so common place to her, she really had no idea how bad it had got.

Today was meant to be a good day, the weather was nice and they were off to a wedding of a family friend. Gerald was not looking forward to it however. He wasn't particularly sociable and preferred to keep his own counsel. Gerald really wasn't a people person. He hated big gatherings.

Annoyingly for him, Sally was calling because she was ready and he wasn't. Perhaps for the first time, she was ready to go out before him and had made a point of calling him every ten seconds. He wondered if she was doing it deliberately but what he did know was, that she now knew how it felt.

Gerald had been ready for ages but as usual these social functions took as much for him to prepare for mentally as they did to dress for. He knew that once he got there he'd probably enjoy himself, but the hardest part would be the getting there. Eventually he casually walked down the stairs, met by Sally deliberately looking at her watch and indiscreetly shaking her head.

"You wait for me when we're going out for a meal or to see a film, those things we can be late for," Sally replied. "We cannot be late for a wedding." She had an answer for everything but despite this Gerald had an incessant controlling urge to have the last word every single time. "Last time I checked Restaurants and Cinema's also work to a specific time and require you to be there at those times, so it's no bloody different." he answered, smugly. Sally couldn't be bothered to respond, she'd seen this Gerald enough times. Today she was going to be stuck with picky, bullying, constantly right even when wrong, Gerald. He had a tendency to suffer mood swings, which was putting it lightly. Sally knew that even if there was the slightest hint of an argument, Gerald would pick it out. She knew he didn't want to go, she also knew he'd be nice and polite to everyone except her, when they got there. After, over twenty years, she was used to it, it was his way. Sally didn't like it, but she loved Gerald and she knew it wasn't his fault, he had a problem. For years Gerald's mood swings had pushed their relationship to the brink. Sally often thought it was because Gerald didn't love her, but in fact that couldn't have been further from the truth. He really did love her and couldn't explain his moods or the way he could be so vitriolic either.

After years of his erratic behaviour Sally urged him to see a Doctor and it was here the diagnosis was made. Gerald was a depressive. He could do little about it other than take vegetative medicine and he definitely did not want to spend his life like that. The only other option was to try and help himself by controlling the way he felt and behaved, which was often easier said than done. Gerald put up with it and so did Sally. Even though he had a problem, living with 'Mr Cranky Pants' as Sally called him, was never easy.

The two of them got in the car, saying very little and drove off.

"Do you know where you are going?" Sally innocently asked?

"No, I'm fucking guessing, let's see where we end up!" Gerald answered with a thunderous look on his face. That was another quirky trait for Gerald's condition, when he was in one of these moods, his profanities reached Guinness World Record levels. Sally knew not to say anything else, it was clear to her Gerald was having a more than bad day.

A short while later, as they hit an A road, Sally glanced over at the speedometer. As it rose from sixty, to seventy, to eighty and then in excess of ninety, Sally became nervous. Irrespective of his mental problems, she was not about to have her life put at risk by one of his 'moments'.

"You are going much too fast" she said. Gerald failed to respond, just sucked his bottom lip into his mouth and sneered.

"Gerald, you're going much too fast." Sally said again.

"Says who?" replied Gerald at last. "I'm in control, the car is fine, why don't you keep your fucking nose out." he said.

"No, I won't, you are driving too bloody fast Gerald and you are making me nervous." Sally answered.

"How the fuck do you know, you can't even drive, what's it got to do with you for fucks sake, fuck off." Gerald said, driving faster.

"Please Gerald, just slow down." Sally said. He smiled. "I thought you were worried about the fucking time we were going to get there." he said, as the speedometer topped one hundred miles an hour.

"You're too close to the car in front." Sally said, just as there was a sudden bang. One of the front tyres blew and in an instant, the car went from travelling in a straight line to being thrown into the metal barriers that ran alongside the road. Sally screamed while Gerald swore, but the car kept going, scraping alongside the barrier, sparks of metal flying into the air. Out of nowhere the barrier ended and the car flew down the embankment at break neck speed, hitting a ditch and rolling onto its side. The rolling didn't stop as both Gerald and Sally were smashed around inside the car. She had stopped screaming and Gerald didn't know why. His anger had quickly been replaced by fear as the car rolled on its seemingly never ending journey, Gerald's head thumping the top of the car with each roll. Surrounded by a screech of tyres and horns, the car abruptly came to a halt, just long enough for Gerald to see the lorry hurtling towards them.

The next thing Gerald recalled was waking up in hospital, his leg and arm in plaster. A miracle, the Doctor had called it. To escape from such an accident with such limited injury had been amazing.

The Police visited Gerald and informed him Sally had been killed. His stomach was filled with total emptiness and the room spun around him before he passed out. The Doctors had told him it was the shock and for the next couple of months, while he recuperated in hospital, he fell into a pit of the worst depression, considering, many times, ending his own life. He never did of course, gutless to the end he figured.

It was near the end of his recuperation that Gerald started receiving calls to his bedside telephone. At first it sounded like incoherent whispers, but then he realised it was actual words. When Gerald deciphered the words as being Finnigan's Point, he looked them up and that was how he came to be here now, sitting in a car with three practical strangers.

The others listened with baited breath as Gerald relayed the whole story to them. It was a tragedy and a terrible thing to have happened, but why after all that, had he been drawn to this place? Nobody knew the answers.

"That's the first time I've told the story in full," Gerald said. "I told the Police the tyre blew and I just lost control."

"Were they OK about that, did they believe your story?" Kane asked.

"Yeah, they did, they had no reason not to, to be honest, the tyre had blown, but I was lying to myself." Gerald said.

"Not really," said Paul. "It was an accident."

"An accident caused by me," Gerald said. "If it wasn't for me I'd be at home now, with my wife, instead she's dead, and its my fault, I killed her." The others looked on as Gerald began crying. Floods of tears ran down his face as Adam patted him on the back. None of them could disagree with him, he was right, it had been his fault. A tragic accident made all the worse by the fact it could have been avoided.

"Want to know why I ended up here?" Adam asked, figuring a change of subject may just take the focus away from Gerald.

Paul and Kane both nodded, they did indeed want to know Adam's story. Gerald continued to sob alone in the corner of the car, while Adam began to relay his tale.

71

Chapter Fourteen

Adam's Story

The rain hammered down outside as Adam sat in the living room watching the TV. He'd been trying to write this book for what seemed like an age and as usual, he was getting nowhere fast. The story had seemed simple at first, your generic serial killer book, but this one he just couldn't get a handle on. In the past few years Adam had become fairly prolific in his writing. He didn't have much of a following and made very little money, but it was enough to get by, most of all he was happy. How many people did he know who worked from day to day doing jobs they loathed, to pay for the lives they owned. Many, was the answer, and he did not want to be one of them. Sitting at the keyboard, again, trying to think of something intelligent and insightful to write. Adam jumped at the sound of a loud bang upstairs. Adam had no idea what the bang was, but as usual he'd slightly spooked himself from his writing and so feared it was some maniac breaking in to get him. He figured probably not, as it was the middle of the day, but you never knew nowadays, there was that much scum on the streets of Britain, it was hard to be sure. Again, a bang sounded out from the upper half of the house and again Adam jumped. The rain was teaming down outside which allayed his fears of an intruder. What kind of self respecting burglar would burgle anywhere in this kind of weather?

Assured there was no intruder, Adam went on to the next possibility and unfortunately for him, the next possibility was a paranormal one. This scared him even more. He totally believed in the after life and was in no way a sceptic when it came to ghosts. Suddenly, the ominous sounds from upstairs turned into a certain ghost, as far as Adam was concerned. He new though, whatever happened next, he'd have to venture upstairs and see exactly what was up there. It was at times like this he'd wished he'd asked his girlfriend, Chloe, to move in with him. He was a bit of a wimp but would never admit having a woman around the house would make *him* feel safer.

Gradually Adam plucked up the courage to venture upstairs, but not before another bang rang out through the house. Slowly, climbing the stairs with legs as heavy as if he'd just finished a marathon, Adam finally reached the top. All looked well. The landing was lit by the light from the bathroom window and the spare bedroom looked fine. All that was left was for Adam to check his own room and it was here the horror waited for him. Not the kind of horror to make a film about, or the kind that sends shivers down the spine, but the kind that made Adam shout out loud. "Oh for Christ fucking sake!" as he opened the door, there he was met by three large chunks of ceiling which had collapsed on the bedroom floor, due to the volume of rain they had taken on from above. Looking up through the hole and into his loft, Adam could see the daylight and the rain coming through his roof. He'd had no idea it was there, or in fact how it had even arrived. How would he though? Until your bedroom ceiling collapses there's little way you would ever know what was going on above it. As far as Adam was aware no one he knew routinely checked their loft. Standing there, looking up into the hole in the ceiling, thinking of the best way to solve this problem, Adam was completely unaware of the loft beam, falling down towards him. He had no time to think or even react as the huge hulking piece of wood landed squarely on his head, knocking him to the floor in a shower of blood and scattered ceiling pieces.

Awaking in the hospital with a searing headache and an inability to focus properly, Adam remembered what had happened. The Doctors fixed him up and before too long he was allowed to go home, fortunately the heavy loft beam had done nothing more than give him concussion and a considerable loss of blood.

Soon after his release from hospital, Adam bought his newspaper, as he often did in the mornings and took it home to read. To his astonishment, various letters had been hi-lighted in bright yellow marker pen, throughout the paper. Sitting there

73

trying to work out exactly what they related to, became a bit of a game to him. Part of him suspected it was some jokers mindless act of needless vandalism, but another part of him wanted it to have a meaning. Adam was a big fan of puzzles, from Sudoku to Crosswords, he loved them all and was exceptionally good at most.

After three days of trying to decipher this 'code' Adam realised that every other hi-lighted letter when pieced together, formed the words Finnigan's Point. Right throughout the paper, the words Finnigan's Point, were spelled out no less than fifteen times. Adam had never heard of Finnigan's Point but assumed Finnigan was a person. Searching the vast space and array of information that was the internet, he came across a place in the outer Hebrides with the same name. On reading about Finnigan's Point Adam decided it sounded nice enough to visit. As he had been suffering fairly severe writers block for some time he decided Finnigan's Point may very well be the best place for him to take a break. So, like Gerald and Kane, Adam had arrived in the town with no expectations and no real reason.

Gerald had stopped crying and all three of the men now listened to Adam's story as intently as they had the previous, it was a mystery.

"Go on then, Detective, work out what the bloody hell is going on, because God knows I ain't got a clue" Adam said.

Kane didn't have an answer and he didn't think Adam really expected one. It seemed impossible, all three of them came from different parts of the country, knew nothing about each other, had no connection whatsoever, yet had all been drawn to this mysterious place by strange and unconnected forces.

"It's impossible," Kane finally said. "We've all been drawn here for a reason, something or someone wanted us here, now we can't escape, but why?" Kane asked, rhetorically.

"Well it's something paranormal, because however fast you drive in one direction, it should take you away from the place you left." Paul said, again looking out of the rear window, still stunned by how close the town remained to them, despite the long drive.

"We have all had near death experiences in one way or another and then ended up here," Kane said. "I can't work out why though," he continued. "We haven't all had near death experiences though have we?" asked Adam. "What about Paul?" They all turned to Paul, waiting for an answer. Paul stared back saying absolutely nothing.

"Go on then Paul, tell us your story, how and why did you end up in Finnigan's Point?" Gerald asked. Paul again said nothing, just shrugged his shoulders. The three men were not willing to let it go. Before Kane arrived Paul had told both Adam and Gerald that he too had been 'drawn' to the place, but had never elaborated on exactly what that meant. "I just liked the look of the place on the internet," he said. "I wasn't told to come here and nothing whispered to me, or called me or finished my bloody crossword." he answered angrily. Kane wasn't convinced, neither were the others, Paul was being cagey for a reason. "Paul, you're not telling the truth." Kane said. Paul took exception to this comment.

"I bloody am!" he said, sounding like he was trying to convince himself as much as the others. "Tell us your story Paul, because I think we all have one and this could be our ticket out," Kane said. "You were the one who said we all had something in common, now prove it."

"OK," Paul agreed reluctantly. "But I'm warning you, whatever is happening here is merely a coincidence, nothing more and nothing less. I don't have a story half as interesting as you guys."

Chapter Fifteen

Paul's Story

The sound of the telephones constantly ringing on and off, along with the senseless chatter of the people answering them echoed around the office.

Sitting at his desk, as usual, was Paul, idly thumbing through a book of blank post-it-notes. His mind off elsewhere, he was interrupted by someone calling him.

"Hey Paul," said Nigel, the blond haired blue eyed boy of the office. Nigel was the one who could never do any wrong and invariably only ever spoke to Paul when there was something to make him look stupid. Paul hated Nigel with a passion. "Got a job for you." he continued, as if Paul had responded to him. Paul looked at him and he could tell by the smug grin on Nigel's face this was going to be no picnic.

"Yeah, what is it?" he asked, neither caring or wanting to know. Nigel laughed, as did everybody else in the office, as though they were in on Nigel's private joke.

"Harold Hill." everybody stopped laughing instantly, the sound being replaced by a few random sniggers. One of the other guys in the office summed up everyone else's thought. "Fuck off!" he said. Paul had been trying to sell Harold Hill for over a year. It had become the millstone round his neck. It wasn't so much that he was a bad salesman, it was the house. It had a well publicised history, particularly locally, there had been no interest in the place at all. They'd had to bring the price down to such an extent Paul stood to get little commission from any sale at all. Nigel had lumped the property on Paul as soon as it had become available, just for the comedy factor Paul assumed. "Is this a joke?" Paul asked Nigel, knowing it probably would be. He was surprised by Nigel's answer.

"Nope, may be your lucky day at last. Some out of towner wants to look around, has a genuine interest in the place. Doesn't sound like some nutty ghoul." he finished. There had been plenty of people wanting to look at the place initially, but all for the thrill factor and never with any intention of buying. The problem with being an estate agent is you have to treat everyone as a potential buyer, whether you have a feeing they are genuine or not. The last occupants of the house had been a normal suburban family. Wife, Husband and three kids. Nothing unusual in that and no reason for the house to gain notoriety over it. That was until the Father butchered the whole family before hanging himself from the loft.

Paul never liked going there, the place felt creepy and cold, whatever the time of year. He figured it was down to the stories which the house was associated with, rather than any real haunting, but you never knew. He'd heard plenty of stories of sightings of people in the windows and sounds of banging and hammering at night. Paul had never heard or seen anything there, he just felt it.

Paul expected his client was no doubt another one obsessed with the macabre, but he couldn't afford to take the risk and so, after arranging with Nigel the time to meet the prospective buyer, Paul went on his way.

The house was only about half an hour away, situated in a small road with a handful of other, practically identical houses.

When Paul arrived a man waited outside. In his early fifties and distinguished in appearance, he stood patient. Dressed in a smart suit, his greying, slightly balding hair swept back, the man smiled as Paul climbed out of his vehicle. Paul introduced himself and had a feeling this man may indeed have a genuine interest in the property. Usually within the first minute of meeting any likely buyer they somehow got round to asking about the murders and the so called ghost sightings. It was at this point Paul realised he was basically a tour guide. This new gentleman though, mentioned nothing of the past and just enjoyed the house.

"So, are you looking to move into this area permanently?" Paul asked.

"Yes, yes I am, it's nice round here, very quiet but not too far away from the hustle and bustle of the town." he replied.

"Where are you currently living then?" Paul asked. He wasn't interested in the answer but found these walk rounds easier if he struck up a conversation. He also had no intention of letting this possible sale go to waste. He'd feel a huge relief if he could get this monkey off his back.

"I live nowhere near here actually," he replied "But I'm looking for a change of scenery."

"Where do you live?" Paul asked him again, continuing his polite but banal conversation. "A place called Finnigan's Point, up in the Outer Hebrides." the man replied. Paul had never heard of such a place.

"Not very nice there then, I assume?" Paul responded.

"On the contrary, it's one of the nicest places I've ever lived, amazing in fact." the man said.

"Odd to leave then," Paul replied "Have you just had enough?"

"As you can outgrow people, you can outgrow places," the man responded "but I would recommend that if you ever want to go somewhere to relax and I mean really relax, then Finnigan's Point is the place to go, there is nowhere more tranquil on Gods Earth." the man continued.

After the walk around, Paul led the man outside and told him to let them know as soon as he could if he was interested in the property, as they had a number of offers and enquiries.

"Please don't offend me," the man said. "I know you've had not one offer on this place."

"What makes you so sure?" Paul asked.

"Because people are afraid of murder, people do not want to live with the aftermath." he answered.

Paul was surprised not once had the man mentioned the history of the house, yet he had known about it all along.

"Personally, it doesn't bother me, what went on in that house is the business of those who lived and died here, all I'll be inheriting is an empty shell, ready to start all over again." Paul couldn't believe his luck, finally it seemed, he was at last going to get rid of the house on Harold Hill, something that seemed impossible only yesterday, Paul couldn't wait to wipe that smug grin off Nigel's face.

"That's great, so you want the house then?" Paul asked.

"On one condition," the man replied. Paul was waiting for the 'under one condition' clause and decided that one condition would end up being the one which prevented him from finally selling the place.

"OK, what condition?" he asked, humouring the man.

"On the condition that should I sign on the dotted line to buy this property, you take a break and visit Finnigan's Point."

Paul was taken aback, he had not expected this. Why would this man care whether he wanted to take a break or not? As if he had been reading Paul's thoughts, he answered that very question.

"You look as though you could do with the break."

Paul shook the man's hand. He was right, what harm would come of it. He'd finally sold the millstone and gained a holiday too. All in a good days work.

"That's it? That's your story?" Adam said, sounding disappointed.

"Yeah, that's it, what more did you want?" Paul asked.

"I don't know, us three are linked by our brush with death and the obscure connections to this place afterwards. I'd kind of hoped you'd have a similar tale of woe, to try and get, you know, a common link." Adam continued.

"I don't think our near death experiences are the link," Kane said. "I think the link is this place and how we have all been drawn here."

"Still doesn't answer why though does it." Gerald said, looking out of the car window. "I think you are all missing the point a little," Paul said. That guy who mentioned this place to me, who bought the house and told me to come here? That guy, he got out, he got out of Finnigan's Point.

Chapter Sixteen

The four men continued to sit in the car for a few more minutes, discussing their situation, how they had all inexplicably been drawn to Finnigan's Point and more importantly, how they could get out.

"What was the guys name, who you sold the house to?" asked Adam. Paul thought for a few moments.

"You know what, I can't remember for the life of me, it's not something I've really thought about since. Why, anyway?" he replied.

"Because we could ask after him in town, see if they know him." Adam replied. "Why don't we just ask one of them in town to take us out of here? They can't all be staying here all the time, they must leave at some point and go elsewhere?"

It was a good idea they all agreed and as Paul couldn't remember the name of the person who bought the house it seemed like the only option. "I've got another idea," Adam said. "Why don't one of us get out of the car now and the other three drive off in the direction of the exit. The one who remains behind can see what happens?" The others thought about it, Kane decided it was a great idea.

"OK as you suggested it, why don't you stay here and see what happens then?" Kane said.

"OK," Adam agreed. "But if you three get out, you sure as shit better come back and find me, or send someone to rescue me."

Kane and the others laughed a little.

"Don't worry, we won't forget you," Paul said. "We'll know where to send a Christmas card as well." Kane said, laughing.

"Yeah, laugh it up you guys, let's see what happens when you drive off." he said, before opening the door and leaving the car. Standing by the side of the road, kicking up the dirt with is shoes,

Adam watched as Paul, Gerald and Kane drove off into the distance.

Adam stood motionless, looking after the car as its diminishing figure eventually disappeared. He was amazed and a little concerned, they had gone, just as simple as that. Standing there for only about a minute more Adam was filled with anger and jealousy. It had been as easy as pie and now he was stuck in Finnigan's Point. He cursed himself for suggesting the idea of one of them leaving the car. Beginning to feel isolated and alone he was suddenly startled by a noise approaching behind him and turned to see the car arriving, as if it had just driven straight out of town.

Kane pulled over alongside him and opened the door. "What happened?" Kane asked "How did you end up in front of us?"

Adam had no explanation, none of them did. It was as if they were trapped in the same place in time, reliving the same stretch of road over and over again.

"It's impossible," said Adam. "What the fuck is going on here!?" The four men couldn't begin to understand.

"This is madness." Kane said, hi head feeling heavy as the enormity of the of what was happening pounded his skull.

"Well, fuck this," said Paul. "We may as well head back to town for what it's worth, we're obviously meant to be staying here."

"I agree." Gerald spoke. The other three jumped mildly at the sound of his voice, he'd been practically silent since he'd told his story.

After it's short and insignificant drive, the car rolled back into the space it had left previously that morning.

"I'm going over to the bar," Paul said, as the others silently climbed out of the car.

"If I'm stuck in this fucking place I may as well have something to eat and a nice cold beer, God knows I don't have to worry about driving anywhere and being pulled over for it." he continued.

"Maybe we can ask in the bar if anybody has trouble getting out of town." Gerald said. The other three nodded, agreeing it was a good idea the four of them made there way back to the bar.

On entering they saw only three people, including the barman, sitting inside.

Two men sat at the bar and both looked at Kane in an inquisitive way as he made his way over to order some drinks.

"Hi," he said to the first man, bearded and dishevelled looking, in his late forties. The man didn't speak, just raised his glass to Kane and then retreated over to a table, with the other guy swiftly following, like an out of sync shadow. Kane pulled out the grubby looking stool and sat down at the bar.

"Four beers please." he said to the barman. The barman nodded in the affirmative, not speaking, looking up, he surveyed Kane and asked "New in town?" as he clinked the four glasses together in one hand, placing them down on the beer stained bar ready to pour into.

"Yeah, yeah I am, just been here a couple of days, nice place." The barman nodded again, concentrating on the beer he was pouring.

"It's a lovely place, but after awhile, it all looks the same, if you know what I mean." the Barman replied. Kane certainly did know what he meant, particularly after today's car ride to nowhere.

"Yeah, I guess it could be," Kane replied. "Do you ever leave town though, get away elsewhere?" The Barman stopped what he was doing and appeared to be thinking.

"No, no I don't, I always stay here, nowhere else to go anyway and at the end of the day, as much as I get fed up with this place, the world ain't gonna make me feel any better is it?" He said.

"Can't argue with that," Kane said. "This world has had it. So you never venture away from here at all?" The Barman just shook his head and then asked for payment for the drinks, holding his hand out over the bar. He felt around in his pockets, before removing the money and settling the bill. As he carried the tray of beers over to his table he noticed the two men looking at him again.

"Ever leave Town much?" he asked them as he walked past their table. Both men looked away from him and began talking to each other as if Kane had interrupted a conversation they'd clearly not been having. He placed the tray of drinks down on the table and sat down. "Nobody here appears to leave town anyway and if they wanted to, I don't think they'd complain too much if they found they couldn't." Kane said to the other three.

"We were just saying how strange it all is," Gerald said. "None of this makes any sense and yet none of us are even remotely freaking out."

"What can we do," Paul said. "We're stuck here until we can find someone who can help us."

"Why don't we just call someone to help us from outside of town?" Kane said. "Great idea Detective, why didn't we think of that?" Adam said, getting slightly agitated. Kane could also feel himself getting flustered. "It' a simple enough question," he said. "I don't see anyone else making constructive suggestions." he continued.

"No signal on the mobile phones and if you ask in the hotel, they don't have one." Paul said.

"What kind of hotel doesn't have phones?!"

"The same one that doesn't have televisions either?" Paul replied.

"We're holidaying in the fucking twilight zone." Adam said.

For the next couple of hours the four of them sat around, talking, drinking and even laughing about the situation they found themselves in, they all agreed there could be worse places to find themselves trapped, but even so, no matter where it was, no one really wanted to be trapped anywhere.

"I'm going to go back," Gerald said, standing up. Kane looked at his watch, just as Adam looked at his.

"It's only ten, why don't you stay a bit longer and we'll all go back together?"

"No, you're all right guys, I'm tired, I'll see you lot tomorrow." Gerald said. "It's OK, we can all go now, eh guys?" Kane said.

"No way, I haven't even started this beer yet." Paul said, gesturing to the full pint currently sitting on the table in front of him.

"Really, it's OK, I'll see you all in the morning." Gerald said, before making his way to the door and outside into the dark night, leaving Adam, Paul and Kane sitting there at the table, none of them displaying any real intention of following him out.

As Gerald walked outside he was hit by the cool air, the temperature had dropped rapidly and for the first time since he'd arrived he felt cold. The wind had picked up also with a breeze sounding like whispers on the air. As Gerald approached the hotel he realised that there really were whispers in the air. "Gerald" it seemed to say, over and over again. A chill ran down his spine as he picked up his pace, the dark of the night feeling threatening to him now. "Gerald" again he heard it and this time he turned around and looked back towards the dense woodland that sat at the end of Finnigan's Point. Gerald could see a shape in white, standing at the entrance to the woodland. "Gerald" again whispered on the breeze and he was sure it was coming from the direction of the mysterious white glowing shape. Tentatively, he quietly walked towards the shape at the edge of the woods. "Gerald" the whisper rang out again. His heart raced uncontrollably. Gerald was now near enough to the shape to make out its form. He wasn't sure but it looked like a person, possibly a woman, shimmering in the dark. Suddenly the shape disappeared in an instant and Gerald picked up his pace to follow it. Again, the now clear and distinct sound of "Gerald" reached his ears and again, it appeared to be coming from the woodland. He could just make out the white light again and continued to follow it, unaware he was being lured deeper into the woods and away from the sanctity of the town. Following the sound and the light for another five minutes he was suddenly plunged into total darkness. With no idea exactly where he was or how to get back to where he'd come from Gerald stood, in total silence and shock, completely unsure of what to do next. The eerie silence of the woods was broken, by the sound of a crack behind him. Sure it would just be an animal, Gerald turned to see what was there, before screaming loudly.

Standing nose to nose with him, it's battered and bloodied face pressed almost up against his own, was the bruised and pained expression of his deceased wife, right before his eyes.

"Hello Gerald, miss me?" she asked.

Gerald stood still, the terror coursing through his body, making it impossible to speak or move.

Sally stepped back and Gerald could see the extent of damage to her, she looked terrible.

"Sorry Gerald, I'm not looking my best am I." she said.

Gerald started sobbing uncontrollably.

"I'm sorry, I'm sorry, I'm sorry." he said, over and over again. Sally held out her hand to him. "I know you are Gerald and I don't blame you, so stop blaming yourself, it was an accident." Sally said.

"It was my fault." Gerald said to her, still crying,

Sally shook her head. "It doesn't matter anymore Gerald," she said, still holding out her hand. "Take my hand please Gerald, I have missed your touch."

Gerald looked at her. "Why should I take your hand, what's happening Sally, why are you here, you're de..... dea....... dead?" Gerald stammered.

"I know, but do you trust me Gerald?" Sally asked, staring at him intently through her lifeless eyes. Gerald slowly nodded his head.

"Of course I do Sally, I always trusted you one hundred percent."

"Then take my hand Gerald, I will take you away from this place, you do want to leave this place don't you?" she asked.

"Yes I do, very much, I want to go home now." Gerald answered.

"Then take my hand and I will take you there." Sally said.

Gerald reached forward and tightly grabbed her icy cold fingers, as she led him deeper into the dark and chilling woods.

Chapter Seventeen

The following morning Kane was awoken by the sound of heavy rapid banging on his door. Half in a sleep induced daze he looked at the clock. It was only just after eight and he had no idea what the urgency was. If there was one thing he'd learned about Finnigan's Point, it was that nothing was ever urgent. Bleary eyed Kane opened the door to Paul and Adam, standing there looking wide eyed and serious.

"What's wrong?" Kane asked

"Gerald's gone," Paul said. "We knocked and he's not there."

"So? he's probably gone for a walk or something," Kane said. "What's the urgency with you guys getting up so bloody early in the morning as well, it's not like we're going anywhere today, is it?"

"He's gone, gone," Adam said. "We've checked with the woman on the desk and she told us he's left, not returning either."

Kane laughed at them. "Really?, well finding him shouldn't be too much of a bloody problem should it, he can't get out of the poxy place either can he." he said.

"That's what I was thinking," Paul replied "and if he could get out, he'd damn well tell us how to as well wouldn't he, he wouldn't just leave us here by ourselves."

"He wouldn't disappear without saying goodbye either." Adam said. Kane shrugged his shoulders.

"OK, so the old dear down there is sure he's definitely gone then, she could have got it wrong, no?" Kane said.

"How the bloody hell can she get it wrong, she has four people staying here, one was in his room and two were talking to her, the chances of her getting it wrong are pretty bloody small!" Paul said, getting annoyed with Kane's blasé attitude.

"Well we can look for him, assuming he hasn't got far, we know he can't get out of town using the road, we tried the twilight zone route yesterday and it sure as hell doesn't work."

Paul looked down at Kane and raised his eyebrows.

"Get some underwear on for Christ sake man." he said causing Adam to look down as well.

"Jesus man, you're standing at the door with your knob hanging out." responded Adam. Kane looked down at himself.

"I thought there was an emergency, it could have been a fire." he said exasperated with them both.

"Well you wasn't putting it out with that mate." Adam said wryly.

"Can I get dressed now please? I'll see you two in a minute." He said slightly embarrassed by not remembering to put on his pants before he opened the door. Paul and Adam left to go and wait downstairs for him while he smartened himself up.

He wondered where Gerald could have gone. There was no way any of them were getting out on the road and less of a chance that Gerald would have tried again, alone, in the middle of the night. Kane thought back to the night before. Gerald had been fairly quiet and left earlier than them. He wondered if he had done something stupid. Remembering the accident which had killed his wife and crippled him with emotion the day before. Matched with their inability to get out of Finnigan's Point and the feeling that they had all been lured there for a reason, He thought there was a possibility Gerald really could have done something silly.

When he got downstairs, he told the others what he thought. It turned out they had been thinking exactly the same.

"Listen, it's not a big place, searching it would take half a day, if that." Adam said. Paul and Kane nodded, it was fairly small, he thought and if they split up they could cover the whole area fairly quickly. But Kane didn't want to split up, he felt safer when he was with the others. He couldn't put his finger on why, he just did. The idea of finding Gerald's body alone, if he had done the unthinkable, was also not top of his list of things to do today. He'd seen his fair share of bodies during his lifetime already and he had no intention of seeing more.

"I think we should stay together, rather than split up." Kane said, feeling silly as he said it. There was about as much danger in this place as a kiddies playground.

"I didn't say anything about splitting up, had no intention to either," Adam said. Paul nodded his head in agreement and he was instantly relieved. His new found friends felt the same as him. The three men aimlessly ambled around the Town, asking various people if they had seen anything of Gerald and from everyone they got the same negative non conversational response. It appeared mostly everyone there had no idea who it was they were looking for and eyed the men with a reluctant and questioning eye. Adam mentioned to one of the townsfolk that the three of them were trapped in Finnigan's Point and got the biggest reaction of the day, uproarious laughter. It appeared as though everyone in Finnigan's Point thought they were mad and the three of them were beginning to feel like they were probably right. Eventually they came to the local grocery store. The attractive lady was serving again, with her customer friendly manner evaporating in to thin air as soon as she saw Kane and the others.

"Can I help you?" she asked, looking directly at Kane.

"We're not shoplifters, you don't need to be so wary of us." he said to her, smiling.

"What is it you want?" she asked him again, in a tone of total disdain.

"I want to know two things, firstly, why are you so unhappy with me and secondly, what is your name?" He said, still smiling. He saw a fleeting glimpse of reaction behind the woman's eyes.

"I am not unhappy with you," she said. "I'm just doing my job, you are the customer and I serve you." she continued.

"And your name?" he asked again, his smile and easy going demeanour never once fading.

"My name is Francesca Sir, and yours?" Francesca said.

Kane was overjoyed just to have got a name out of her, it was a start. If he was going to be stuck in this town then he may as well try and strike up a conversation with the most visually stunning woman he had ever laid eyes on. "That is a lovely name," he said. "Unfortunately mine isn't. Terrence Kane," he said, holding out his hand "pleased to meet you". It was as though the touch of another human being was all that was needed to crack her icy exterior.

At last, she smiled. "Terrence is a very distinguished name, and I too am pleased to meet you." she said.

He thought about his next response, he hadn't expected her to want to talk to him and wasn't thinking about his next move. "While I'm here, it would be a shame not to take you out to dinner," he said. "Would you like to join me for a meal?" Francesca didn't say anything for a short while, just stood there, thinking seriously about her response.

"OK," she finally said. "I would like that I guess."

Kane couldn't believe his luck, the ice queen had turned into the fair maiden in one fell swoop. "That's great, do they serve food in the bar?" he asked her. She nodded. "I'll meet you there at seven?" OK Terrence Kane, I will see you there at seven." she replied. "Sorry to interrupt this romantic interlude," Paul said. "but we have to find our friend."

"I shall see you later." Kane aid to Francesca as he turned to leave with the others. "What's happened to your friend?" she asked as the three men began to leave the store. "Nothing" he said. "Just playing hide and seek."

Once they were outside Adam started to laugh.

"Unbelievable, we can't find Gerald yet you manage to get that miserable bitch to smile AND arrange a date with her, I've no choice but to have some respect for that!" Adam said.

"Us two loners will sit on a table away from you tonight and enjoy a laugh at your expense." Paul said, oozing jealousy.

"Laugh it up girls," Kane said, "You two are just devastated because you didn't ask her and I can't blame you."

"I'll ask her after tonight," Adam said, "She'll be sick of you by tomorrow." Paul was looking ahead, still laughing, when his smile faded and his walking drew to a halt.

"If you really think he might have committed suicide, then there would be the place to do it," Paul said, pointing in the direction of the woodland. "Any amount of places to hang yourself from in there." he continued "Yeah OK, enough of the graphic images thanks," Adam said. "I doubt he would have done that anyway Paul, but we should go and check I suppose, cover all the bases and all that."

Kane wasn't so sure and was the most apprehensive of all of them.

"No, no, I doubt he'd be in there." he said.

"We're checking though," Paul said, starting to walk in the direction of the woods.

"I'm not going in there," he said, "I'll wait for you guys here."

"No way!" said Adam. "You said you didn't want to split up and you're meant to be the bloody detective as well, so you're coming with us, no choice."

Kane still stood in the same spot, apprehensively. He didn't want to go into the woodlands and with good reason, but he wasn't about to tell these two why.

"Come on," Paul said. " They won't bloody bite you, its just trees for Christ sake!"

"It's not that, I just don't like woods, I haven't been to the woods since I was a kid, bad experiences." He said.

Now Paul and Adam were intrigued and clearly wanted to know more. What could possibly drive a grown man to an irrational fear of nature?

"Go on then, what was the bad experiences, elaborate?" Adam asked.

"None of your business, just leave it and know that there is a good reason I'm not a big fan of the woods." Kane said.

"Grow up will you man," Paul said out of the blue. "Whatever happened to you when you were a kid isn't going to happen now, come on, lets have a quick check and see if we can find anything in there."

"We've run out of options," Adam said. "This is about the last place for us to try and find Gerald and if he's not in there, then fuck it, somehow he got home and maybe he'll send someone to find us, OK?" Reluctantly he nodded his head in agreement. He'd seen some repugnant things as a detective but still, nothing frightened him so much as a walk in the woods. He knew to the others he looked pathetic and usually that would be enough for him to put on a brave face. In this case, he didn't care how he looked, he was too wrapped up in how he felt. As the

90

three men walked towards the overgrown trees and bushes that made up the entrance to Finnigan's Point's picturesque woodland, neither Adam or Paul, pushed Kane for the reason for his phobia. He was glad, because there was no way he was going to tell either of them, no matter how much they pressed him for an answer.

Reaching the opening to the woodlands, Kane drew in a deep breath. It had been some time since he'd been anywhere like this, but he figured Paul was right, he was a grown man and needed to act like one. He decided that if there was a time to face his fears, then now was it.

"OK," said Paul. "Let's look in here and hope against hope that all we find are some leaves, some birds and some fucking berries."

The three men walked into the woodlands, looking like age old novice explorers all at the same time.

Kane wasn't happy being in the woods, but with the others, it didn't seem as bad or claustrophobic as he'd anticipated. He guessed perhaps there was a method to the madness of facing your fears. Walking further into the woodlands, leaving the town behind them, none of them saw anything out of the ordinary, but it was a vast space and would take them an age to check the whole of the woods.

"This is ridiculous, we're not going to find anything in here, he hasn't bloody killed himself anyway and if he had, he wouldn't have ventured in this far to do it." Adam said. "Why wouldn't he?" asked Paul, equally perturbed by their seemingly pointless search.

"Because he'd want to be found, most suicides want to be found, otherwise why do it?" Kane asked. He had a point of course, if Gerald really had wanted to kill himself, he would have wanted his body found, of that they were all sure. Just as they were about to call a halt to the search and turn back, Paul spotted something up ahead, just catching the corner of his eye.

"What's that through there?" he asked, pointing out in front of himself. Adam and Kane both looked, neither of them seeing anything at all. Paul walked on ahead of them and then they both laid eyes on what it was Paul had seen. There, in a small clearing up ahead, sat a lone cottage. From the outside the white building looked fairly immaculate. There were no other houses around it and to get here wasn't the easiest of routes. It was cut off from the whole of town, totally alone.

"Funny place for a house wouldn't you say?" Kane said. The other two nodded in agreement, neither saying anything.

"Well let's go and see if anyone lives there." Paul said, walking ahead of the others. He strolled up to the red front door and knocked loudly against the solid wood. Waiting, al three of them knew there would be no answer. Paul knocked again, the rapping of his knuckles echoing around the vast area of woods surrounding them.

"Nobody home." Paul said, to himself as much as anyone else.

"Well I'm not surprised, hardly the most convenient of locations is it." Adam said in response. Kane walked around the outside, looking at the house. Unlike his compatriots he wasn't so sure.

"I don't think this place is vacant, somebody lives here." he said. Paul and Adam looked at him for an answer, but with his hand on his chin, Kane began to ponder again. "Why are you so sure?" Paul asked, scratching his cheek. "Well look at it, it's immaculate, someone is taking care of this place. It's not just sitting here to decay, someone lives here." he said again. Adam went up and looked in one of the windows. He could see furniture inside and the place looked well kept. Inside was neat, tidy and well organised.

"He's got a point," he said, "It looks pretty well lived in from where I'm standing."

Paul knocked on the door again, jumping back as it opened with the rap of his knuckles. "Jesus, was that opened just now?" he asked the others, trying to peer through the crack between the door and the frame. "Must have been," Kane said, but not really sure as he edged past Paul. He was itching to do some detective work again and figured this could be a good place to start. "Lets go in." He said. Much to the surprise of the other two.

"And what? Burgle the place?" Adam said. Paul laughed.

"No, snoop around see who this place belongs to, like you say, it's odd being here all on its own like this, you two can become honorary detectives for the day." he smiled.

"Ooooh," Paul said sarcastically, "Almost worth breaking and entering for." Kane just laughed.

"The door was already open, I wouldn't say that means we're breaking in, we're just checking everybody is OK in here." Kane said.

"No harm in it I suppose?" Paul said. Adam wasn't happy but by default had been outnumbered by the other two, so decided it would probably be easier to go along with them.

Kane quietly pushed open the door, struggling to quell the ever increasing memories of Mr Donovan mercilessly shooting him.

The three men stood in the doorway, cautiously looking around. The room was split in half, with the kitchen and dining room on one side and the living room on the other. A tasteless art nouveau decoration covered the walls and the room looked modern yet dated at the same time. The air was filled with the distinct smell of Potpourri.

"Anyone home?" Kane called. There was no answer, as he'd expected.

"We're like Goldilocks for fucks sake," Adam said. "Lets just go, we won't find anything here anyway." Again Paul and Kane ignored him, opting instead to go on a self operated tour of the house.

There was nothing out of the ordinary at all. A single bed in the double room was about all the three of them could find of any use. Clearly, whoever lived here, lived alone.

"It's obviously being lived in, but there's definitely nobody around at the moment, Adam's, right, we should probably leave, there's nothing of any use to us here." Kane said. The three men finally agreed and one after the other left the house.

"What should we do about Gerald?" asked Adam as Kane closed the front door behind him. "Nothing much we can do, just hope he's either coming back, or has found a way out and is getting help for us." Paul said. "You know it is feasible he's just fucked off and gone, I mean he didn't know you lot and certainly me all that well. He owed none of us a thing." Kane said. "Yeah, but he'd tell us if he found a way out." Adam responded, unimpressed by Kane's theory.

"Maybe, but what if he tried to get out again and actually got out. If it was you, would you run the risk of turning back and coming into town again to tell us lot?" said Kane.

"Yeah, I would." Paul lied. Adam and Kane both laughed at this, knowing full well that he wouldn't.

"Yeah, like hell you would." Adam said, Paul didn't respond.

Walking back through the woods the three of them agreed to call of the search for Gerald. It was getting late and there was little point in any of them thinking they'd find him. They were starting to believe he really had got lucky and found his way out.

Eventually, on finding the exit from the woods, they made their way back into town. Kane was pleased he'd faced his fears. He decided the woods weren't that bad after all and he also thought with that out of the way, he should go and get ready for his date with Francesca.

As Paul, Adam and Kane made their way up to the hotel, none of them saw the hooded figure, dressed in black, watching them from deep inside the woods.

Chapter Eighteen

The fluctuating temperature of the shower drove Kane mad. Just as he thought he'd got it right, in a jet of erratic bursts, he'd find himself semi scalded. Leaving the shower, he looked at himself in the mirror. He was met with the sight of a blurred and cloudy reflection. The heat of the shower had steamed up the entire bathroom, he felt as though he was drying off in an eighties music video.

He left the bathroom and looked at himself in the bedroom mirror. The scarring around his chest from the gunshot had been fairly minimal. Not only had he escaped death, but he'd escaped permanent unsightly damage as well. All in all, he'd got off lightly.

Having no idea how long he'd intended to stay when he left home, he had packed a fair portion of his rather limited wardrobe. He was happy he had enough clothes with him to at least afford the opportunity to not only wear something different for his date with Francesca, but something smart as well. Thumbing his way through the items hanging from the misshapen metal hangers in the hotel wardrobe, He finally settled on something simple, but always effective. A crisp white shirt and black trousers. Most clothes suited him, he was lucky in that respect. He could shop for clothes and come home with an assortment of items from various unconnected shops, everything he brought back would look as though it was made specifically for him. He could be known to walk around in a shirt and tie, just as easily as he could a pair of bright Bermuda shorts and Hawaiian shirt. One of the traits of being a detective was an ability to fit in absolutely anywhere, he was certainly able to do that. He was the archetypal square peg in the round hole on many occasions and always seemed to pull it off. Looking at his now dressed self in the mirror, he felt assured he looked smart, sophisticated and dateable, at least he hoped he did.

The disappearance of Gerald had concerned him, just as the oddity in being unable to leave the town had the day before. Despite these two things, there was something intoxicating about Finnigan's Point, to such an extent, matters that would seem phenomenal and important elsewhere, felt minimal and insignificant here. He couldn't put his finger on what it was that Finnigan's Point had, that kept him intrigued, yet not enough to really put his detective hat on.

Right now, his main focus and his number one priority was meeting Francesca at the bar. He was unhappy the only place to socialise was the same place everyone else would be, including Paul and Adam, but he knew beggars can't be choosers and just getting Francesca to agree to a date was achievement enough, not to jeopardise over the location of choice.

Spraying himself liberally with aftershave and wiping the remains into his hair, he took one final look at himself in the mirror. Smiling at his reflection, he left the room, locking the door behind him.

Walking down the wood lined corridor, he breathed in the familiar smell of pipe smoke drifting down the length of the corridor, fading the further he walked. He guessed Gretna Greene's husband was probably about at last. As he approached the reception, there sat Gretna, knitting something that at present, resembled nothing more than a piece of woven wool. He gave her a quick smile, which she readily returned, causing the wrinkles on her face to fold enough to age her by a further ten years, if at all possible.

As he left the hotel, he was surprised by the sharpness of the night air. It was cold, bitterly in fact, as if the season had changed in the space of a day. Looking up he could see the night sky aglow with millions of stars. Seeing the stars above always made him realise just how insignificant he was and not just him, everyone. He often wondered how many people took the time to really think about how they'd got there, and how the earth had been fashioned. It was all too easy to believe in a God, he'd always thought that. For him, choosing a being as the sole purpose behind life's creation was nothing but a cop out. As far as he was concerned, the Bible, and all he read in it, was nothing but fiction. Good fiction, but irrelevant and no more worth basing your whole belief structure on, than a Harry Potter book. He often laughed at the prospect of kids waking up on December 25th in a thousand years time, to be greeted by gifts delivered by a wizard on a broom stick. All he really believed was that life was created by science and things he was not meant to know about. He didn't knock peoples beliefs, it was not his place to do so. Kane strongly felt nobody had licence to decide who was right or wrong on that front. Looking at the stars and the infinite possibilities that emerged from them, held a sense of real calm and euphoria for him. Breathing in the cold air he cold sense the universal smell of rain, as it hits the soil and sure enough, he felt the first drops of rain he'd known were coming.

The rain started to fall fairly hard as Kane picked up his pace and made the short journey to the bar. As he approached the door he took one more look up into the night sky, rain splashing his face as he did so. It was almost as if he'd been followed there by an invisible cloud, the sky was still completely clear.

Entering the bar he was disappointed to see Francesca was not there. Paul and Adam however were, sitting drinking their beers and talking to each other. Neither of them noticed him as he walked in, engrossed in their conversation. He took one more quick look around, Francesca wasn't there. The bar was fairly quiet, apart from the occasional clink of glasses and nondescript chatter at the bar as people ordered there drinks.

Kane made his way over to the table Paul and Adam were sitting at and joined them.

"Bond in the house," Adam said, laughing. "You going on to the casino after your date with 'Miss Baggytits' Mr Bond?" Paul laughed, Kane however didn't, just sat there looking serious.

"What the bloody hell is 'Miss Baggytits'," he asked Adam.

"I dunno, sounds like a bond girl don't it?" he said smirking at his joke.

"Sounds like a Bond girl who's about eighty yeah." Kane said.

Paul looked around the bar, loosely followed by Adam, searching himself. "You been stood up?" he asked, looking at his watch.

"Actually its early days yet, don't give up hope." he continued. Adam was laughing. "Yeah, don't give up yet, she only said she'd go out with you so that you'd piss off and leave her alone." Adam said, still laughing at himself. "Yeah, maybe but either way, she spoke to me, which is more than she did to you." Kane replied.

"She's spoken to me," Adam said, indignantly. Kane was laughing now. "Yeah, when?" he asked. Adam was looking sheepish now.

"She told him how much his groceries were," Paul laughed. "You can stay with us if she don't turn up." he continued. "What have you guys been discussing anyway? Kane asked. "What do you think we've been talking about, the weather?" Adam said, looking miserable and fed up. "What's your problem snappy?" Paul said.

"I don't know, maybe being stuck here for all eternity, maybe Gerald disappearing into the fucking Bermuda triangle, what do you reckon?" Adam replied, still snapping.

"There's no point going over the same old ground, Gerald's gone, we're stuck in this bloody place and right now, we can't do a thing about either." Kane said. Paul nodded in agreement. "Some Detective you are, no wonder you got shot." Adam said. Kane was starting to get angry, Adam had no right to speak to him like that.

"We won't get out of here if we don't stick together, that I know for sure," Kane replied, looking at Adam. "and Since when has it been my fucking responsibility to get you out of here? Maybe you should take a leaf out of Gerald's book and find your own way out." he continued, raising his voice enough to cause people in the bar to stop and look round at the three of them.

"Listen guys, this isn't helping is it," Paul said. "We're all pissed off and fed up, but we're not going to find any answers taking it out on each other."

"How are we then, nobody here seems to have a brain cell between them, we can't reach the outside world, there's no TV here either, which, if you ask me is the strangest thing of all, so please explain, where are the answers?" Adam finished. "I'm hoping Francesca will be able to answer questions, there must be a way the townspeople get out, otherwise how do they get supplies and provisions?" Kane said.

"Well good luck with asking her those questions, she's not even going to bloody turn up." Adam said.

Just as he finished his sentence the door to the bar opened and there, in a smart black dress, stood Francesca, looking radiant.

"Is she not now?" Kane smiled sarcastically, as he rose to leave the table.

"Best of luck with that, for all our sakes." Adam said, begrudgingly. Paul nodded, in sincere agreement, as Kane walked over to Francesca.

"Evening," he said to her, smiling. I was beginning to wonder if you were going to turn up." he said. Francesca attempted to crack a smile herself. It was apparent that smiling was not something she often practised. "I was beginning to wonder myself." she said. Kane led her over to one of the vacant tables and pulled out the chair for her to sit down. Breathing in he could smell the soft flowery scent of her perfume. Francesca was like a summer breeze with legs. "Would you like a drink?" he asked her, still standing. Francesca thought for a moment. The choice in the bar was typically limited and required less thought than she was giving it.

"A dry white wine please." she finally responded. Kane walked over to the bar, catching the glances of Adam and Paul, who both nodded towards him, Paul raising his glass.

Francesca sat alone at the table, quietly looking around. Paul and Adam watched her while Kane ordered the drinks. She acted like someone who'd never been in a bar before, taking in every sight as if it was her first introduction.

Kane returned to the table with the drinks.

"Thank you. Your friends are watching me." she said. Kane looked over to them both and rotated his hand clockwise in the air, to suggest they both turn around and concentrate on their drinks.

"They're just intrigued by you, they think your cold, miserable and rude, they are a bit surprised you agreed to come out with me and to be honest, so am I," he remarked. Again Francesca tried to smile and again it appeared to be a struggle.

"That's totally unfair really," she said. "I'm a lot more than just cold, miserable and rude, I'm also bitter, spiteful and unkind." Finally she smiled in a natural and unforced way. Kane smiled too. He'd been wondering what this 'date' would be like, particularly as he knew absolutely nothing about Francesca, other than she was beautiful but slightly unapproachable. "How long have you been single then? he asked. "Seems odd to me someone like you would be, particularly in such a small town."

"Have you seen the men around here?" she replied. "I've been single for just about as long as I can remember."

"Well, I guess that's just lucky for me then isn't it" Kane said.

"We'll see how you feel after this evening, then you may not feel lucky at all." She replied, laughing. She seemed to have changed her persona suddenly. Her shoulders had relaxed and she looked less like she was waiting to have her toe nails pulled and more like she was willing to enjoy herself.

"What brings you to Finnigan's Point anyway?" she asked him. A good question, but one Kane could hardly answer with the truth. "Just fancied a break really," he answered. "This place looked nice on the internet and I figured it would be worth a visit, and it is nice, but a little strange." He continued. "How is it strange?" she asked, looking puzzled. "Well you know, it's lovely and quaint and a cracking place to relax, but it's also a little, you know, 'Wicker Man' Kane said. Francesca's puzzled expression didn't lift. "Wicker Man, what does that mean?" she asked, running the tip of her index finger around the top of the glass as she did.

"I don't know, just a bit different. I'm used to a lot of traffic, noise, lights TV, Internet, telephones, just daily things. This place is more like an ancient untouched village." Kane finished, taking a gulp of his beer. Francesca smiled again, relaxing him. Up until that point Kane wasn't too sure if he was offending her or not. "I see," she answered. She sipped her wine, looking at Kane over the top of the glass. 'I see' he thought to himself, what kind of response was that. He decided she really couldn't 'see' at all. Deciding to let that conversation rest, he decided to change the subject slightly.

"So how long have you been here?" Francesca shuffled in her seat, again appearing to think to deeply for a response to a question that didn't need an in depth answer.

"All of my life, I was born here, I grew up here, I will end my days here too." she responded. Kane was a little taken aback by her reply. As nice as Finnigan's Point was, there was a very final feel to her answer and he couldn't help but think there were other much better places she'd never see because of it.

"That's a shame," he said. "You should venture out more, there's a whole World out there waiting for you to go and see it."

"Yes, maybe, but as you said, it's noisy, bright and busy and none of those things appeal to me." she said. "I can also see myself staying here forever as well." Kane said. She smiled.

"Really, so you like it that much?" Kane didn't have the heart to tell her what he really meant. Although he'd witnessed how none of them could get out of town, he still felt stupid saying it out loud and so again chose the simple answer. "Well, at least as long as you want me here anyway." He answered, in an unbearably sycophantic tone. "We will just have to see how it goes then won't we?" she smiled. "But it's good to know your future fate rests solely in my hands." she laughed. "Wouldn't want it any other way," Kane replied, smiling at her. "Would you like to order some food now?" Francesca looked at the menu. "Hmmmm, what to choose, what to choose!" she said sarcastically. There were not many options, in fact if you didn't like jacket potato you were going to get a sandwich. Both choosing a jacket potato, Kane again made his way over to the bar to order, noticing both Paul and Adam had finally had the decency to retreat elsewhere. It was now he who felt relaxed. He hadn't realised it, but sitting there with Paul and Adam's eyes boring holes in his back had been rather off putting. He was glad not to have to sit there for the remainder of the evening, like a caged animal on display at the zoo.

Over the course of the meal and the evening, the two of them conversed with meaningless chit chat. They talked about themselves without giving anything away and revealing anything significant, but enjoyed each others company. He was reasonably sure Francesca liked him and he definitely liked her. Having gone into the evening intending, if nothing else, to find out what she knew about the town and to get her thoughts on his current dilemma, Kane had asked and decidedly little. Eventually the evening drew to a close and both Kane and Francesca made their way out of the bar. "I'll walk you home," Kane said, as they found their way into the brisk chilly air. "Its cold." he said. "It's freezing, always does get cold here in the evening due to the water," Francesca answered. "and yes, you can walk me home, its only a three minute walk away anyway." Kane was pleased she wanted him to walk her home and was also intrigued by her comment about the water.

"I'm surprised this small lake can affect the temperature so much." he said, as the two of them walked away from the bar and hotel.

"No, no," she replied "The sea, just over there." she signalled towards the woods. Kane looked in the direction she pointed. He had absolutely no idea there was sea in that direction.

If there was sea, then there was another way out.

"I'm surprised, I hadn't the faintest idea there was sea anywhere near here," he said. "I came off a main road to get here. There was no sign mentioning sea in any direction."

"Oh yes, if you follow the woods all the way to the end, they dip down to a small beach, it's all there," she said, "There's a lot more to this place than meets the eye." Kane couldn't disagree with that, he'd been fooled by Finnigan's Point more than once already. Francesca stopped outside a small bungalow.

"This is me," she said. "Thanks so much for a lovely evening."

"Thank you," Kane said. "I've had a nice time getting to know you and finding out you're not so cold and heartless after all." Francesca leaned forward and kissed him on the cheek.

"Give it time, I may just be the coldest most heartless person you meet." she replied, laughing. "Goodnight Terrence." she said, making her way up the short cobbled path towards her front door.

"Goodnight Francesca, perhaps we can do this again before I go?" he said. Her smile was clear under the automatic porch light which lit up as she approached it. "Go?" she said. "You said you would be here forever!" she laughed as she closed the door behind her.

"I better not be." Kane said, under his breath as he walked away, back towards the distant light of the hotel.

Kane looked at the darkness which surrounded him and back at Francesca's house. He suddenly felt immensely alone and was very aware of how close he was to the woods. Going in there during the day was a different ball game to the dead of night and he knew he wanted to get back to the hotel as soon as he possibly could. On the breeze, so faint it was barely audible, Kane thought he'd heard his name whispered, as he briskly walked away from the woods. Again, as he neared the hotel, he thought he heard his name whispered on the breeze and then as suddenly as it had arrived, the feeling of dread left him and he entered the hotel, relieved. Back in his room he looked at himself in the mirror one last time before undressing himself and making his way to the bathroom. After cleaning his teeth, he switched the lights off and briefly glanced out of the window at the total blackness which now shrouded Finnigan's Point. Leaving the window to climb into the warmth of his bed, Kane hadn't noticed the only faint light in the distance, moving gently and soundlessly in the depth of the woods.

Chapter Nineteen

"Jesus Christ, where'd he go?" Chris said, looking into the hole left by Harvey's fall. Terry looked in, mouth agape. After seeing the woman standing near the so called witches house and now Harvey's apparent disappearance,, it had been a fairly shocking five minutes.

"Are you guys going to help me or what?" a voice said, from way down in the hole. Chris and Terry quietly looked into the hole and both burst out laughing, in good humour as much as relief. There, laying at the bottom of a seven foot deep hole, covered in leaves from head to toe, lay a dirty and dishevelled Harvey. He didn't look happy. "Ha, it's always you, isn't it." Chris said, chuckling.

"Yeah, and it's always you two sticking together and laughing at me, are you going to help me out of here or not?" Harvey asked again. "No, you're OK, we'll leave you there." Terry said, laughing.

They helped Harvey clamber out of the hole with some difficulty. Standing there, brushing the mulch and leaves off, he smeared something wet and brown down the front of his shirt. "Oh, you guys, this better be mud." he said, lifting his hand to his nose. Harvey gave his fingers a little sniff and his reaction was enough to leave Chris and Terry doubled over with laughter again.

"It's bloody shit!" Harvey exclaimed, dancing around wiping his hands on the leaves all around him. "I'm covered in shit." he said again, while Terry and Chris struggled not to wet themselves with laughter. After five minutes of franticly rubbing his hands over everything he could find, Harvey was satisfied most of the excrement had gone, off his hands at least. "I can't believe my luck, it gets worse by the day" Harvey said, standing there looking as though the weight of the world was on his shoulders. Terrence patted him on the back. "Never mind, Harv, you smell a bit that's all, probably fox poo". He said. "Yeah, and you always smell a bit anyway." Chris said, rubbing it in a little bit more. "Yeah, thanks, you're really funny you are." Harvey said. "Listen guys, we should head back." Terry said. "Get out of it, we haven't been here long." Chris said, looking upset at the prospect of leaving so early. All he had to look forward to when he got back was a smack round the head from his Dad and an argument between his parents. He was in no rush for either. "I saw a woman there down by that witches house." Terry said. It was Harvey's turn to start laughing. "You're such a wimp, as if there was a woman down there." he said, pointing at Terry as if to confirm who he was calling a wimp. "Shut up retard," Chris said. "What happened then, who'd you see?" he asked Terry.

"Oh, I'm a retard," Harvey interrupted. "If I'd said I saw a woman down there you'd both be laughing at me right now and calling me names, can't win can I?" He was right of course, that would have been exactly what happened.

Chris and Terrence had an understanding and a good friendship.

They'd been playing football outside late one afternoon, after school, Terry was waiting for his Dad to come home from work and even though he wasn't sure what time it was, he knew it was late for his Dad. The Police had arrived soon after and the rest of that day had been a blur for Terry ever since. His Dad had been killed in an accident on the way home from work. A lorry driver had fallen asleep and careered across the duel carriageway, killing six, including Terry's Dad. In the wrong place at the wrong time, that's what everyone had said, but it was no comfort to him. Eleven years old and growing up without a Dad, taken from him out of the blue and for no reason. Terry had watched his Mum encase herself in an emotional shell since then and even though he hoped there was, part of him knew from that moment on, there could be no God. What type of God would take a child's Father from him so cruelly?

Throughout the whole of that period, Chris had been ever present, always there as a friend and a protector. Kids at school could be cruel, and say stupid insensitive things to Terrence, but Chris was always there to take care of him, to defend him.

"I saw a woman, I'm not making it up Harv, I saw her standing there." Terry said. "OK, maybe, but it was probably just someone else visiting the woods or something." Harvey said, looking a little uneasy now.

"Yeah, could be, but something didn't feel right, I was scared" Terry said. "Well either way, she's gone now, so why rush off?" Chris said. "We've got to shoot the gun off as well, we're not coming all the way down here with that and not using it."

Terry had forgotten about the gun and was hoping he wasn't the only one. He felt crafty taking it and even though his Dad wasn't there to tell him off about it, he could almost feel him scolding him through the trees. "OK, I'd forgotten about that, we'll use the bullets we've got but then we have to set off home, it takes longer to walk here than I thought." He said.

Putting the bag down on the ground, he opened it and pulled out the gun. It was the first time Chris or Harvey had seen it out of the bag, both gasped in awe of it. "Cool," Harvey said, reaching for it. "Can I have the first shot?" Terry thought for a moment.

"Yeah, OK, why not, we've been giving you a hard time all day, you can have first go." he said, passing the gun to Harvey. He looked shocked that he was holding it, and pointed it in the direction of the others. "Jesus Harv, point it the other way will you!" Chris exclaimed. "It's heavier than I thought it would be," Harvey said, looking down at the gun in his hand, "and cold too. What shall I shoot guys?" he asked, looking unsure. Chris spotted a squirrel running up one of the trees.

"Squirrel up there." he said, pointing in the direction it was running. "Oh yeah, I see it," Harvey said, pointing the gun in the squirrels direction, while trying to pull the trigger. "It's hard to squeeze." he said, as a bang rang out. The bullet went somewhere, but nowhere near the squirrel. Harvey fell back on the ground. Terry and Chris looked at him, wide eyed. "It's OK, it's OK, bloody loud though ain't it." Harvey said, the others started laughing at him.

"My turn," Chris said, snatching the gun from Harvey's reach. "Lets see if I can actually hit something this time, instead of wasting the bullet like Harvey."

Looking around, Chris spotted another squirrel sitting in the distance and took aim. Again a bang rang out throughout the woods, and again the squirrel ran off. "Something wrong with the sights on that thing." Chris said, annoyed with himself. "Yeah you're the gun expert," said Terry, taking the gun from him. "I'm not firing at anything living." He aimed the gun at a discarded R. Whites lemonade bottle, some distance away, propped up against a tree. Again the bang rang out through the woods, again the squirrels ran and the birds flew. The bang was met with a shattering of glass, as the bottle exploded into a thousand pieces, scattering the woods with glass. "Good shot, good sho.t" Chris said, genuinely impressed. "Yep, the sights are out." Terry replied, grinning.

"Yeah, good shot, that glass will probably kill more animals than a single bullet would have done as well." Harvey said, sarcastically. "How many goes left?" Chris asked. "I want to beat your bottle hi.". Terry opened the gun and had a look. "Only one left, I should have that as its my gun." he said. "Come on, you've already hit something with it, let me have another go." Chris said, reaching for the gun. "What about me, don't I get a say in it?" Harvey asked, also reaching out. "How about we just toss a coin for it?" Terry asked. "I'll call against Chris, Harv you do the same and I'll call against you, overall winner gets the last shot, fair?"

They all nodded.

Terrence threw the gun down on the ground as he reached into his pocket for a coin. As the gun struck the surface it went off, firing the last bullet. Terry jumped out of his skin as Chris started laughing.

"Oh well, no need to toss for it now!" Chris said, looking at Harvey. Terry glanced at Harvey, laughing himself, just in time to see the gaping wound where Harvey's left eye used to be, blood pouring down his face as his body collapsed back and landed on the ground with a thump. Harvey's lifeless right eye looked up at the sky above him. He was no longer worried about the leaves all over him, he was no longer worried about anything at all. Terry sank to his knees as a pool of dark red blood spread out behind Harvey's head, soaking the leaves.

"No, no, no, no! " Terry said over and over again, his head in his hands. Chris stood open mouthed, tears streaming down his face, staring at Harvey's body, the wound in his face where his left eye had been, filling with blood.

An hour later, Chris and Terry sat with their backs to a tree, looking at the lifeless body of their friend, who lay where his soulless shell of a body had dropped the moment the bullet had hit him.

"What are we going to do?" Chris finally spoke. "We killed Harv, what are we going to do?"

Terry looked at him, his face white as a sheet. "It was an accident." he said, his eyes glazed over and tired.

"But we killed him, what are we going to do, what are we going to say to his Mum and Dad, what's going to happen to us Terry?" Chris said, shaking.

"I don't know, I really don't know." Terry said.

Kane sat upright in bed, his body glistening with sweat. The clock said 3.04am.

"Fucking dream, fucking poxy dream, just leave me alone,, please, leave me alone". he said to himself, laying back down. Staring at the ceiling, Kane knew, despite his efforts, he wouldn't be getting any more sleep that night.

Chapter Twenty

The sun's rays cut through the curtains, leaving a rainbow of colours on the wall of the room. Kane lay in bed, looking at the contours of the artexed ceiling. If he looked close enough, he could make out what appeared to be faces, hidden within the patterns. The dream of the previous night had shaken him up and he couldn't get back to sleep.

After a quick shower he was ready for the day. After last night's date with Francesca he'd had an idea and was waiting to let Paul and Adam know about it. Walking across the corridor, Kane knocked on the door adjacent to his own. Paul answered and Kane could see Adam sitting in a chair in the room. "How'd it go last night?" Paul asked, bleary eyed. "Went well, she's a nice lady, we got on OK, I think we may go out again." Kane replied.

"I don't give a shit about that, did you find out anything about this damn town?" Paul asked.

"Hungover?" Kane asked him. Paul nodded his head, slowly.

"We got absolutely wasted last night, Adam trashed his room and had to stay here, old Gretna is going to shit a brick when she sees it." Paul said.

Adam continued to sit in the chair as Kane came into the room.

"Lets hope she don't kick me out because I can't leave this fucking town can I?" Adam said, clearly feeling sorry for himself.

"Why'd you wreck the room?" Kane asked him.

"I don't know, too much to drink, lost my head." he replied, looking sheepish. "That's great isn't it, that poor lady down there is going to have to clear up your shit then is she?" Kane said angrily.

"Don't start, I've had it in the ear from him all night." Adam said. Kane laughed at this picturesque statement.

"That what you charged him for staying in your room?" Kane asked, looking at Paul. "Very funny, now, anything good come out of last night?" he enquired again. "Actually, there may be, yes, she was telling me the sea is just beyond the woods." he said, looking pleased. "She didn't mean the lake?" Adam asked. "No, she meant the sea, real sea." Kane answered, still looking pleased. "OK, so what's the point then? There's sea, so what?" Adam said. Kane didn't have an answer to that one, Adam had a point.

"Perhaps we can buy a boat or something, get out of here that way, the sea will lead somewhere." Kane said hopefully.

"Yeah, I've seen a boat shop here haven't I?" Adam said sarcastically. Kane was starting to get angry with his negativity.

"Well at least I found out something productive, rather than staying here and smashing the fucking place up!" Kane shouted.

"OK guys, calm down, we can go down there at least and you never know, maybe a way out for us, let's not piss all over the idea straight off, OK?" Paul said, Adam nodded, reluctantly.

"Lets go then." Kane said, eager to get down there.

"We will, we will, but first of all, we need to try and clear up the mess Adam has made of his room before Gretna finds it and turfs him out."

The three men got up and left the room, taking the short walk down the corridor to Adam's room. Opposite it was the room Gerald had stayed in. The three of them looked at Gerald's door and said nothing. Adam unlocked his door and threw it open, standing back to survey the damage. Everything in the room was as it should be, untouched and untarnished. The room was as clean and spotless as ever. "Where's the problem?" Kane asked, looking around. Adam and Paul both stood there, open mouthed. "The place was fucked, totally done in!" Adam exclaimed, still looking amazed by what was in front of him. "He's not joking, it was a complete state." Paul said, looking as stunned as Adam. "So Gretna heard the noise, came up to see and gave the room a tidy." Kane said. The others were not satisfied by that explanation. "I smashed things to smithereens, there's nothing broken now, its all whole"

110

"Well then she replaced them with spares, maybe out of Gerald's room or something?" Kane said. Adam wasn't convinced. The three men made their way downstairs and there at the desk, as ever, was Gretna Greene. Adam couldn't resist saying something to her.

"Hi, sorry about the noise and mess last night, it won't happen again and if you need any money for the damages, let me know."

Gretna looked at him with her vacant smile. "I have absolutely no idea what you are talking about dear," she said. "I didn't hear or see anything last night, apart from you two guys come in quietly and go up to your rooms." Adam nodded and walked away, looking at Paul and Kane with an expression of bemusement.

Once outside he went to speak.

"This ......".

Paul immediately interrupted him. "Don't say it, we know, this place is fucked up!"

As the three men approached the opening to the woods, Kane felt the same nervous apprehension he'd had the day before. He couldn't help his fear of the woods, what had happened to Harvey when he was a kid, had scarred him for life and he'd never got over it. He'd never been even remotely close to a woods of any sort since that day.

Standing there, the others looked at Kane, waiting for an answer. He looked at them and then pointed off in an easterly direction.

"It's over that way, somewhere." he said, still pointing.

"How bloody near is it?" Adam asked. "Are we going to be walking all day?" "I didn't ask how near it was, but by the way Francesca spoke, it wasn't far." Kane replied. "Great, well lets hope not." Adam said. "Stop bloody moaning," said Paul. "you've been tetchy since you got up this morning."

"Hangover, I feel like shit and now we're going hunting for sea shells." Adam said, Kane smiled.

"We could be hunting for a way out as well, so why don't you stop moaning and come along and see."

Twenty minutes into the woods and away from the direction of the seemingly abandoned house from the day before, they

111

appeared to still be no nearer the sea. "How near can this so called sea really be, I haven't once heard the sound of waves?" Adam said, still complaining. "It's strange how you don't hear or see any animals in here," Paul said. "I don't even think I've heard a bird sing since we've been walking."

"Yeah, that's true, I've heard nothing either," Kane said. "But then how much can you really hear over this guys non stop moaning?" he said, prodding Adam in the shoulder as he did.

"Hang on, hang on, I hear something, shhhh, listen." Adam said. The three men stopped together and listened closely. As sure as a summer breeze, the sounds of crashing waves could be heard ,not far off in the distance. As they continued to walk, Kane could begin to smell the familiar scent of sea salt, filling his nostrils with every single breath. "That's a fantastic smell." he said, as the three of them plundered through the forest with real purpose now.

Suddenly light shone through an opening and all three of them knew that was their exit to the sea, they could all so readily smell now.

Racing through the gap in the trees, they were met with the sight of a vast ocean as well as soft, silk like yellow sand. There were no pebbles in sight, the place looked like paradise lost.

"This whole beach looks completely untouched, it's amazing." Kane said, Paul and Adam stood alongside him, nodding in agreement.

"OK, we're here, now what?" Adam asked. "You two good swimmers?"

Kane walked onto the sand up to the edge of the sea. Stooping down, he placed his hands in the water. It was cold, despite the sunshine shining on it. Placing his hands to his mouth he took a small taste.

"It's salt, it's definitely sea water."

"So what does that prove then?" asked Adam. "It proves there is a way out, all sea leads somewhere else, we're not trapped in a dead end." he replied. As he stood up, looking at the other two, something to his right, further down the beach caught a ray of sun and glinted in his eye. Looking up towards it, he smiled, then laughed. "Oh, guys, this may just be our lucky day." Paul and Adam looked up the beach, in the direction Kane was staring.

There, just a couple of hundred yards up the beach sat a lone rowing boat, just big enough to get the three of them in.

"We're saved!" Paul shouted, running up the beach towards the boat.

The white boat looked well kept. A set of oars sat in the bottom and the boat itself sat untied on the beach, just waiting for them to take it.

"We should definitely do this" Kane said. "All we need to do is keep close to the coast and follow it, we'll soon find another place away from Finnigan's Point."

"I'm up for it, I have to get out of this poxy town, it's driving me mad." Adam said. "I'm definitely for it too," said Paul. "This vacation has taken too long already and it's time to end it."

The three guys proceeded to pull the boat along the sand and to the edge of the water. Kane was the first to get in, followed by Adam and then Paul. The boat bobbed up and down in the shallow waters edge.

"Anyone know how to work one of these things?" Adam asked, picking up an oar. "You're in safe hands guys," Paul replied, "Champion rower, we'll be fine." He picked up both oars, placing them in the designated slots on either side of the boat. "Seat belts on guys, here we go!" he said, rowing gently. "Seat belts, I could stand up and still be OK." said Adam.

The boat slowly drifted away from shore, as Kane and Adam sat watching Paul steer the boat away from Finnigan's Point.

The smell of the sea rose in the air, it was invigorating as was the sound of the waves crashing around the boat.

"You two ever have a recurring dream?" Kane asked, randomly.

"Sometimes, yeah I do. I have this one about garden gnomes coming alive and hunting me, why?" Adam asked. "Are they after you now"?

"Seriously, since my accident I haven't stopped having the same dream, only it's not a dream, it's real." Kane said.

"How can a dream be real, that makes no sense." Paul replied.

"I mean, it's real events. Things that have happened to me, mapping themselves out in sequence, in my head," he replied. Neither Adam or Paul spoke, they both sat there listening intently.

"I keep dreaming of an event in my life, every now and then and each time I dream it, the dream carries on from where the last one left off, like a soap opera." he said, waiting for them to start laughing. "That's impossible." Adam said. Paul continued to pump the oars, saying nothing. "What's the dream about?" Paul asked. Kane didn't want to tell them, Harvey's death was something he hadn't thought about for years. Blocking it out had taken a long time and now he was thinking about it again, it upset him. He wasn't happy to discuss it with two people he hardly knew.

"What it's about is irrelevant, it is strange though. I just wondered if anything like that had happened to you guys." he said.

"We're not going anywhere." Paul said suddenly, looking back at the shoreline. Adam and Kane stared, Paul was absolutely right, they'd hardly moved at all. "For fucks sake, what is this poxy place!" Adam ranted. Kane was getting used to this and started laughing.

"What on earth are you laughing at?" he asked, as Kane continued to laugh. "Nothing, it's just obvious isn't it, why we can't leave?" he said, looking at Adam and Paul. "Really? Well please enlighten us." Adam said, still angry. "Something drew us all here and now we've arrived, we can't get out. Nobody here seems to believe us, or seem concerned, maybe instead of trying to find a way out, we should be trying to work out why we were brought here. We're here for a reason and the sooner we find that out, I think the sooner we can leave." Kane finished. "Great, well best of luck with working out what our bloody purpose is, nothing happens in this place so how the hell can we find out why we're here?" Adam said.

"If you're right and we have to serve a purpose before we can go, then fine, lets get to work on that, but that doesn't explain what happened to Gerald does it?" Paul said.

"No, it doesn't, I agree, but maybe whatever Gerald was brought here for was done," Kane said. "I'm not saying I'm right guys, but what I am saying is trying to get away from this place is not going to work for us, so we may as well get used to that and look at another avenue." he continued. "Fuck this, I've had enough." Adam said, suddenly jumping into the sea. "What the hell is he doing"? Paul asked, as Adam bobbed up and down in the water. "Well, if we aren't going anywhere, then none of this is real is it, because if it was, we'd be going somewhere wouldn't we?" Adam started swimming away from the boat. "I'll swim out of here." he said, moving further away still.

"Swim where?" Kane asked, "you may be able to swim further than the boat seems to be allowed to take us, but where to, you don't even know what's out there."

Kane looked up ahead at the rippling waves. As far as the eye could see was skyline and an endless depth of blue sea. Kane's eye line was suddenly interrupted by a movement in the distance. Focusing on the area, he was instantly aware of what he was looking at. A fin broke the surface and in a smooth, scarily accurate line, cut through the water, heading forward in their direction.

"Jesus, look!" he exclaimed, Paul immediately spotted what Kane had seen. "A fucking shark in these waters?" He said. "That's not possible!" "This place deals in only the impossible," Kane replied. "ADAM GET BACK TO THE BOAT NOW!" he shouted. Adam raised his hand out of the water, followed by his middle finger, unaware of the fast approaching shark. "WE'RE NOT JOKING, THERE'S A FUCKING SHARK HEADING IN YOUR DIRECTION." Paul screamed at Adam, who now looked behind him. He could make out the fin in the distance himself.

"Fuck me" he said, as he frantically began to swim back towards the boat. Taking in water both through his mouth and nostrils as he desperately tried to get back to the boat in time, Adam could almost sense the beast below, speeding through the water,, ready to pounce on him. Kane and Paul said nothing, just watched helplessly. From their position both of them could see Adam still had an advantage, but it was getting smaller by the second.

The boat seemed an endless distance away for Adam, as if he was getting nowhere near it. His legs ached, his arms hurt and his chest burned. A huge wave rose up from below him causing him to think that the end was coming. Instead the force of the water threw him forward and within touching distance of the boat. Throwing his arms over the side, Kane and Paul dragged him into the boat, just as the shark arrived. Adam lay in the boat, gasping for breath, while Kane and Paul stood open mouthed, looking over the edge of the boat.

A twenty foot Great White shark circled the boat. It's huge hulking frame gracefully moving through the water, causing barely a stir.

"We get sharks in our waters, but not those." Kane said, fixated on the shark as it continued to circle them.

Adam finally mustered the energy to peer over the boat, before falling on his back again.

"Jesus Christ!" It's jaws." he said, lying still. Circling the boat once more the shark disappeared as quickly as it had arrived, leaving them alone once more.

"That was a close one," Kane said. "I thought you was a goner."

"You did? How do you think I felt, I just shit my pants guys." Adam said, lying still. "You got lucky there," Paul said. "What the bloody hell was a shark like that doing in these waters, it doesn't make sense."

"That's Finnigan's Point." Kane replied. "It's like the Rubiks Cube of holiday destinations."

"What the hell is that?" Paul exclaimed, looking towards the shoreline. "Oh God what now?" Adam asked. Neither Paul or Kane had the answer. "Just looked like a black mass standing there, could be anyone." Suddenly a huge splash from behind distracted them. There, its head half poked out of the water was the Great White, seemingly looking at them with its black soulless eye. Just as quickly it ducked under the water and left. The three guys watched as its dorsal fin disappeared into the distance. The figure had gone when they turned back and the boat had drifted surprisingly near to the waters edge. Rowing the remaining distance the men jumped out of the boat and pulled it into shore. "I wonder who that was watching us?" Paul asked, not expecting an answer from the other two guys. "Could have been one of the townsfolk," Kane mused, "Either way, probably nothing important. I'm more interested in that Great White," he continued, "It's unprecedented."

Adams wet clothes clung to him as the three men walked through the woods, back to the sanctity of the strange town. The few townsfolk watched them as they walked through, a couple of them smiling as Adam traipsed along like a drowned rat.

Climbing the stairs to their rooms they were just about to go their separate ways back to their rooms when they were interrupted in the hall by a creaking sound. Turning round Kane noticed the noise was emitting from the handle of Gerald's room, slowly turning. Suddenly the door swung open to reveal a large overweight man, with thick rimmed glasses and a balding head. He looked at Kane and the others, "I thought I heard something." he said, looking at them through glasses which were making his eyes look twice the size they actually were.

"Who are you?" Paul asked, in a tone which suggested he wasn't too pleased to see this new face.

"Tony, Tony Wilson." the man said, offering his hand to shake.

"Here we go again." Adam said, as the three men stood there surveying the new guest.

Chapter Twenty-One

Kane stood in his room, looking out of the window. The trees on the outskirts of the woods slowly moved in varying directions, disturbed by the light breeze. The brief introduction to Tony Wilson had revealed little about him. He was an insurance broker, had a wife and a child and stopped at Finnigan's Point while on his way elsewhere. This was to be an overnight stop for Tony, he had no intention of staying any longer. Apart from that he'd told them very little. Paul had asked him if he wanted to come out with them for the evening, over to the bar, which of course was the only place they could socialise in Finnigan's Point.

Still watching as the breeze disturbed everything, right down to the dandelions, who's delicate flower spread its angel like dust like a small cloud of smoke, into the air, Kane was interrupted from his day dreaming by a knock on his door. He enjoyed nature, even the simple aspect which everyone took for granted on a daily basis and was annoyed by the interruption. He opened the door to reveal Adam standing there. "Can I come in?" he asked, looking miserable. Adam hadn't been happy since this morning, his escape from being a sharks dinner had not helped. It had been a strange day so far, to say the least. Kane ushered him in, he went and sat on the end of the bed. "Nothing that happens here is normal is it, I mean, when you look at it, everything that happens to us here is completely out of the ordinary." Adam said, staring out of the window. "Well yes, we've already established that ten fold, it's a strange place and we're stuck here and that thing this morning, with the shark and the hooded figure, all surreal," he replied. "But right now, there's nothing we can do about it, we just have to hope we can get out of this nightmare."

"Yeah, let's hope we can, but I don't know, I feel like we're going to be trapped here forever, its starting to drive me insane." Adam said, still staring out of the window. When he turned to finally look at Kane the tears were rolling down his cheeks. "You OK?" Kane asked, knowing full well that he wasn't. "I wasn't entirely truthful earlier with you, I have had a recurring dream, pretty much since I got here, only it's the same one, every night." He said, looking at the floor. "OK, well at least I'm not alone and I know your dreaming has something to do with this place, I'm sure of it." Kane said. "Even though it started before I actually came here, I know it's all tied together somehow. Maybe we can get the answer from our dreams?"

"I don't see what answer I'm going to get from mine, it disturbs me and makes me feel ill every time. I don't think I've had a full nights sleep since I got here. It's as if this place taps into your worst nightmare. Being eaten by a shark is one of my all time favourites." Adam explained. "Being eaten by a shark is a lot of peoples all time favourites, ever since the movie Jaws," Kane replied. "What's your recurring dream about then, why do you think you keep having it?" he asked Adam. "I'll tell you, but keep it between us because I don't want anyone else knowing about this." Adam said. "How bad can it be?" Kane asked, sitting on the chair at the dressing table. "About as bad as it could get." Adam replied, looking solemn.

Adam's Nightmare

Adam awoke to bitter cold. He'd opened his window during the night because it had felt quite warm, but this morning it was absolutely freezing. Jumping out of bed, he looked out of the window. To his surprise it was frosted up and outside there was a fresh layer of snow. No wonder it was so cold. Not once had the weathermen predicted snow. He wondered how much they got paid to predict the weather. He could think of no other job, other than Government, where you were paid and not sacked for continuously getting things wrong.

"Great." he thought. Had he known, he'd have got up earlier. He had to get to the publishers early this morning as they were preparing to launch his new book. Knowing the British public's inability to cope with anything adverse weather wise, he knew the snowfall would add another hour to his journey. The main roads would be fine, but he had plenty of rural roads to cope with first. As this snowfall was clearly unpredicted Adam had an idea the gritters were also as surprised as him when they awoke this morning.

Quickly getting showered and dressed Adam was out of the house in half an hour. It was colder outside than he'd thought. As usual, he had no winter preparation and therefore had no idea where his gloves or winter coat were. Throwing on his light, flimsy and predominantly useless jacket, he had no choice but to make do.

Underneath the thick layer of snow covering the car, sat a nice thick sheen of ice, like an extra layer of glass. "Great!" he said again. Unlocking the car he then proceeded to stand there for the next few minutes trying to prize the drivers door open. It was frozen solid and subsequent attempts at all the other doors provided the same result. His hands now red raw and his ears feeling like they were about to drop off, he ventured back inside to boil the kettle. He knew that throwing boiling water over the windscreen would no doubt shatter it, compounding an already miserable morning, but he figured that pouring it down the area of the drivers door may free up enough ice to get the thing opened.

Sure enough, a couple of boiled kettles later and he was sitting inside his car, which felt colder than it did outside. Opening the glove compartment and moving aside the empty chewing gum wrappers, burger cartons, parking stickers and various other things most people would place in the rubbish bracket, Adam found his sturdy plastic ice scraper. Removing the old gum stuck to the end of it, Adam was ready to brave the cold again and try to clear the igloo surrounding his car. Switching the ignition on and getting the heaters going before he started to scrape the ice, Adam got to work. The car was old, rusty and not particularly well looked after, but it always started first time and had been reliable since day one.

Despite the engine running and generating some heat, the car took longer to defrost than he had hoped. Cold frost emitting from his mouth, ears on fire and fingers and toes completely numb, he looked at his watch, he was definitely going to be late.

Climbing back into the car, engine running, Adam put on his seat belt and drove away. The windows were still steamed up and wiping his hands over the inside of the window Adam sped down the narrow road which his house was situated on. Wiping the window did little to help his impaired vision but still Adam drove on, while waiting for the mist to clear. Suddenly there was a loud thump. As there were many fields surrounding the area hardly a day went by without seeing one or more foxes lying dead in the road. Hunting may have been outlawed but irrespective of that, nobody could stop the cars continuing to keep the fox population down. Pulling over and putting his hazard lights on, he jumped out of the car. In the crisp snow and freezing fog Adam could see nothing. Looking at his watch again he figured the injured animal would have probably crawled off to die somewhere. Having one more brief and less than thorough look, Adam got back into his car. Just as he was about to close the door, something red caught his eye, over to the left side of the road. Not sure what it was Adam got back out of the car.

Walking over to the red item on the road he found a small child's coat, with toggles. Looking around he could see nothing else. "Shit!" he exclaimed. Now he didn't know if he had run down a fox or a child. Looking at his watch again, he couldn't leave. Standing there silently in the snow, listening to see if he could hear anything, the only sound the constant clicking of the blinking hazard lights.

A few yards up ahead he spotted a shape, lying in the snow, slowly walking over to the object he was greeted by a small child, a girl, lying there in the snow, unconscious and bleeding from the ears and nose. Her red bobble hat askew and her equally red dress bunched up around her, she lay completely still. But for the blood pouring out of her she looked peaceful and serene. Adam put his hands on his head. A small strangled sound arose from his throat, erupting into a scream that echoed down the cold lane and around the empty fields. Where had she come from? There were hardly any houses near by. He sat down beside her and checked her wrist, there was no pulse. He checked again, frantically, but still could find no sign of life. Looking at her young angelic face he felt like he was about to vomit. Unlike his own breath that filled the air around him, there was only stillness from her. Adam sat with her for what seemed like an eternity, staring blankly across the fields.

Eventually, climbing back into his car, he drove back home, leaving the child's body where he had found it.

It was here that he always woke up.

Adam sat on the end of the bed, tears rolling down his face. "I didn't mean to do it, it was an accident." he said, seeming to apologise to nobody. "You left her there?" Kane said, unsure if that is what Adam had done. "I left her there, I phoned nobody. I left her there to be found." Adam said, looking at Kane with despair and shame in his eyes. "Jesus, that's terrible." Kane said, he didn't know how to react. Adam had killed a child, albeit accidentally, but had knowingly left her there alone. "How was she found?" he asked. "Her Dad went out looking for her, she'd gone out in the morning to play in the snow and had wandered across the fields, he found her body, it was all over the local news." Adam replied.

122

"You got away with it?" Kane asked. "If you can call it living, living with it every day since, getting away with it, then yes, I got away with it." he continued. "Don't judge me, you wasn't there, I panicked, you are the first person I've ever told."

"How do you feel now you've spoken about it?" Kane asked.

"Just as mortified, but like a weight has been lifted. I know what I did was wrong and I pay for it up here daily," Adam said, pointing to his head. "I just wish I could tell her I'm sorry."

"So you've been having that dream recurrently since you got here?" Kane asked. "Yeah, practically every night, what do you think it means?" Adam responded. "It means nothing, it's just your conscience getting to you, when did this happen?" he asked.

"Six years ago this winter, six years, she'd be sixteen now." Adam said.

"Six years is a long time to relive something like that, let's see how you sleep tonight, now you've got it off your chest".

"Yeah, we will see, but this guilt won't ever go away." Adam responded. "Maybe not, but you've taken a step towards making it easier. We all make mistakes Adam, it's how we deal with them afterwards that's the true test." Kane said. Adam nodded his head, looking out of the window again. "I wonder what this Tony's story is?"

"We will find out tonight, hopefully" Kane replied. "What's the betting he's been lured here in just the same way we were."

Chapter Twenty-Two

"It's nice here." Tony said, as the four of them walked down to the bar. "Oh yes it's great here, bet you feel like you could never leave." Paul said half smiling. "Nope, one night stay, I told you. I'll be off first thing in the morning." Tony replied.

"Out of interest, how did you happen upon this place, it's not exactly well signposted is it." Kane stated. "No, no it's not, but I've heard of it before, so knew it was coming up, I just caught sight of the signpost for it otherwise I would have ended up driving right past it." Tony responded "Lucky eh!"

"Yeah, very lucky, your luck certainly was in." Adam said, sarcastically. Tony gave him a strange look, knowing there was some vitriol in Adams statement. "What was meant by that?" he asked.

"Nothing, you'll see." Adam answered, smiling to himself now.

"Is this some game, you lot seem a bit strange, if you don't mind me saying." Tony said, looking puzzled.

As they entered the bar, nobody paid him any attention. Paul ventured over to the bar to get the drinks, while the others sat at the table. "So really, why are you here?" Adam asked Tony. Tony again looked confused and perplexed by what was going on. "Listen guys, I don't know if this is some kind of joke, but I've already told you why I'm here, there's no story." he replied, getting mildly agitated.

Paul returned with the drinks and sat down.

"He's still insisting he just turned up here?" Paul asked the others, as if Tony wasn't sitting right there.

"He is!" Tony answered. "What the hell is going on here?"

For the next couple of hours, Paul, Adam and Kane, went on to tell Tony their stories, how they had been drawn to Finnigan's Point and the things that had happened to them since they had arrived there. "Absolutely insane, the lot of you," Tony said, laughing. "I've never heard anything like it before in my life, a town you can't leave, indeed." he said, laughing at them. "You think it's funny, try it now, go and get in your car and try it now, see how funny you find it when you can't get out of this fucking town!" Adam responded angrily. "I'm not trying this stupid game now, I've been drinking and the only place I'll go is to the hospital, or worse," Tony said, as he rose unsteadily from the table. His legs wobbling he held onto the table as if his life depended on it. "I'm going back to my room." he said indignantly, before staggering and swaying to the door.

Once he had left the other three started laughing.

"For a big boy, he sure can't hold his drink." Paul said.

"He seemed genuinely unaware of Finnigan's Point in the same way we had been before we came here, perhaps he is telling the truth?" Kane declared. "No way. He's been brought here, the same way we have, he just doesn't realise it yet, but he will in the morning, when he can't get out of this God forsaken town." Adam said morosely.

"We will have to make sure we are up early to witness the look on his face when he realises he's just as trapped as we are." Paul said.

Later that night, when all of them were tucked up in bed, Adam as per usual, awoke with a start. The dream had come to haunt him again, only this time, when he got out of the car to check, there really was nothing there. No red coat, no bloodied child, nothing, just the sound of a voice calling his name, across the snow lined fields.

He climbed out of bed and was shocked by how cold the floor felt under his feet. The temperature had obviously dropped during the night, but even so it was very noticeable. Walking over to the window, still sleepy, Adam was stunned to see the grass covered in snow.

"Impossible." he whispered to himself, it was far too early in the year for snow. The view from Adam's window wasn't quite as picturesque as the view from Kane's. Now he was awake, Adam figured slipping his dressing gown and slippers on and taking a quick walk downstairs to see if his eyes were deceiving him, was the least he should do. Putting on his dressing gown

125

and slippers Adam looked at the clock. Two thirty in the morning, perfect time for a wander, he mused to himself. Leaving the room and creeping down the corridor, he could hear the sound of snoring coming from all three rooms he walked past. The alcohol had knocked the guys out it seemed.

Reaching the bottom of the stairs and the empty reception area, he opened the door. It occurred to him that the door was always unlocked, despite there being no one on the front desk. They were either very trusting or very stupid in Finnigan's Point. He hadn't worked out which yet.

As the door opened, the usually warm reception area was filled with chilling cold. His eyes hadn't been deceiving him, he stood and looked at the blanket of snow which covered Finnigan's Point, making it look like a picture postcard. The scene in front of him really could have been the cover of a Christmas card. Just as Adam went to go back the sound from his dream greeted him. "Adam" it called. He stood still, frozen to the spot. "Am I still dreaming?" he asked himself. Again, the calling of his name. Adam pinched himself, it hurt. Slowly walking outside, the cold biting his flesh through his dressing gown, he looked around. He could see nothing, other than the snow. The voice called his name once again and Adam was sure it was definitely coming from outside. A light caught his eye, over by the woods, it seemed to be moving side to side.

"Adam," the voice called again, he was convinced it was coming from the direction of the strange light in the woods. Having grown up a fan of horror movies, he knew the thing to do was close the door and go back up to his room, perhaps waking the others to let them know what was going on. He closed the door, only instead of retreating back to his room he remained outside, the door now shut behind him. The sound was drawing him to it. Adam couldn't help himself, he had to find out who was calling his name. Deep down he knew it probably wasn't the best choice, but being a fan of all mystery and puzzles, he couldn't help but walk towards the disembodied voice. Now trudging through the snow, unaware of how cold he was, Adam walked towards the strange light and the voice, which continued to periodically call him. As the snow soaked through his slippers and numbed his feet, he continued to walk, fast approaching the edge of the woods. He could still see the light but it appeared to be deeper inside the woods than it had first seemed.

Entering the woods he continued to follow the light, his adrenaline pumping, his heart rate soaring and his breathing deep. Suddenly the light disappeared, encasing him in total darkness. His inquisitive nature was replaced with fear. What was this?

"Hi Adam," a voice said, from nowhere. "I'm here." it said again

He looked around, unable to see anything other than darkness and the branches of the closest trees. "Adam, I'm here, you're not looking properly." the voice said again. He continued to look around, genuinely frightened. He'd never felt as alone as he did right now. "I can't find you, where are you?" he asked, in a shaky voice.

"You never were very good at finding me were you?" the voice said. Suddenly from above him, a light brightened the woods. He looked up to see, sitting there in one of the trees, a young girl. She sat there grinning at Adam. Her black shoes dangling from the ends of her swinging legs, her red coat securely fastened and her red bobble hat sitting atop her head. With a grey face, coloured only by the blood running from her ears and nose, she waved at Adam.

"Found me!" she exclaimed. Adam stood, open mouthed, unsure if he was awake or not. "Oh God," he said. "It's you!." The little girl started to laugh. "My name is Alice." she replied.

"I'm sorry, I'm really sorry," Adam said, beginning to weep. "I didn't mean to kill you, it was an accident."

Still smiling, like the cat in Alice in Wonderland, she laughed again. "Can't be late Adam, can't be late." she said, looking at a non existent watch on her wrist.

In an instant she was immediately standing in front of him, looking up at him. He jumped back as Alice held her hand out to him. "Come with me Adam, we can't be late, we will miss the tea party if we do, you wouldn't want to miss the tea party would you?" she said, still smiling.

Adam stared at her, not knowing what to do next. "I'm sorry, I can't come." he said, turning to walk away.

"Oh but you must," Alice said. "If you want me to forgive you, then you must, I am here to help you Adam, come with me." she held her hand out still.

Turning round again, he looked at her. "Is this why I'm here, is this why I was brought here?" he asked.

"You've been brought here to come to my tea party Adam, there's an empty chair waiting for you. You have to come, the Mad Hatter will be so disappointed if you don't." she said.

"Can I go home afterwards?" he asked, petrified of the ten year old girl standing before him.

"You will go home Adam." she said, holding his hand.

Following her into the darkness, Adam disappeared out of sight, swallowed by the darkness and the trees.

Chapter Twenty-Three

Kane walked out of the hotel room exactly the same time Paul did.

"Good morning," Paul said, "Let's go and watch Tony on the road to nowhere."

"Adam coming?" Kane asked, making his way over to Adam's door to give him a knock. "Don't worry about him this morning, he could do with the sleep. He was a grumpy bastard yesterday and after the amount he drank last night I don't think he'll be any better today." Paul replied. "Yeah, you're probably right." Kane said, "We'll tell him what happened when we get back."

"We don't need to tell him, we will have Tony with us.!" he laughed.

The two men knocked on Tony's door, but there was no response.

"Perhaps he already went?" Kane said, just as the door opened.

Tony was standing there in a pair of oversized white boxer shorts, scratching his head, eyes half open. "What time is it?" he asked in a croaky voice. Paul and Kane both laughed. "Ha, not a good drinker then?" Paul said, laughing. "I feel like shit," Tony said. "I've got to get a move on though, I have a meeting this morning. I should never have let you lot get me that drunk listening to your bloody stories."

"Don't rush yourself, you won't be going anywhere this morning." Kane said.

"Oh, that's right, the road that doesn't let you leave, a good'un that!" Tony said, rubbing his eyes. "I'll tell you what, come in while I quickly get ready and then you lot can come and see me off. If you're lucky you'll be able to see me laughing at you in the rear view mirror." He said, laughing with his croaky voice.

Paul and Kane walked into the room. Of course it was exactly the same as theirs. They sat down in the two chairs and waited while Tony literally had a quick wash and got dressed, inside a record breaking five minutes. "Bloody h ell, don't you shower?" Kane asked him. "No time for a shower, I've got to get a move on." he replied.

"But you look like shit." Paul said. Tony raised his eyebrows. "Thanks, but I'm fine." he replied, spraying deodorant on top of the previous days. "He can have one in ten minutes, when he gets back." Kane said, laughing.

The three men walked downstairs, passing Gretna on the way and into the small car park. "You guys coming with me or taking your own cars?" Tony asked. It's just that I'm actually leaving and don't fancy taking you two on the entire journey with me."

"Don't worry about us, as you leave town we'll jump out of the car and wait for you to come back to us." Paul smirked

"Oh yes, that's right, I'm going to end up back where I started. It's an amazing story guys, I cant wait to see it in action." He replied, shaking his head.

Getting in the car, he leaned over and opened the passenger door. Kane got in, leaning back to unlock the rear door for Paul, impatiently waiting outside and trying the handle every two seconds, until it was unlocked. "Jesus, Tony, for somebody on the road, this is one old car." Paul said. "Does me fine." he said, starting the engine. Driving out of town and beyond the welcome sign, he brought the car to a stop. "OK guys, out you hop, I didn't want to drive too far away from town before I let you out, I figured neither of you would fancy a long walk back." he said, laughing.

Paul and Kane got out of the car and stood by the road.

"Thanks for the entertainment guys, I'll see you around." Tony said, smiling. "Yeah, in about five minutes." Paul said, raising his middle finger.

Tony pulled away and drove off into the distance.

"I can't wait to see the look on his fat face when he realises we were telling the truth." Paul said. Five minutes passed and still Tony's car hadn't returned. "How long did it take when you stood here and waited for us to get back?" asked Paul.

"Not this long." Kane said. The sun was beating down hard and even though it was early, he could already feel his neck burning. Another ten minutes passed before both men realised that Tony wasn't coming back. "How the hell did he get out?!!" Paul exclaimed, still looking down the road, like a lost puppy searching for its owner.

"Perhaps we can all get out." Kane said, staring in the same direction. The two of them looked at each other and then turned to run back to the hotel. Racing up the stairs they banged on Adams door. "Get out of bed, get out of bloody bed!" Paul screamed through the door.

Gretna Greene climbed the stairs, her frail old body moving faster than it should have been able to.

"What on earth is all this racket boys?" she asked.

"We're just trying to get Adam up out of bed." Paul replied.

"Oh, he's gone, checked out last night." She said, smiling now.

"There's no way he would have checked out last night." Kane said. "He wasn't in a fit state to go anywhere, he was smashed.!"

"Well I must be making it up then." she said, turning to go back down the stairs.

"Where the bloody hell did he go?" Kane asked. Paul shrugged his shoulders. "Listen, we don't have time for this, if he's gone then good luck to him, that old dear has no reason to lie to us." Paul said. "We need to jump in our cars straight away and see if we can get out of here now".

Jogging back down the stairs the two men made their way to their cars. "Adams car has gone." Kane said. "I could have sworn it was there when we came out this morning?"

"Well it can't have been." Paul replied. He held his hand out to Kane. "This could be it mate, we're going home!".

"Well if we are, shouldn't we bring our bags with us, and perhaps check out.?" Kane asked. "Fuck it!" said Paul, gripping Kane's hand firmly. "It's all replaceable, I just want to get out now and so do you." Kane agreed, they had more than outstayed their welcome.

"OK, let's go, but I'll follow you and the first greasy, dirty, roadside cafe we come to, let's pull over and celebrate finally getting out." Kane said.

Climbing into their cars, they both pulled away, Paul at the front. In a convoy of two, Paul and Kane drove out of the town and joined the road that they hoped would lead them back to the main road and the real world. After ten minutes of driving past the same scenery like a chase scene in a Scooby-Doo cartoon, both men realised they were going nowhere. Paul stopped his car and jumped out.

"FUCK!" He screamed at the sky, slamming his fists down on to the top of the car. "This is a fucking nightmare." He groaned.

Kane climbed out of his car and looked back at the town, just a minute behind them. "Tony got out, we saw him and where's Adam gone?" Kane said, "there's a way out, you know it, we've seen somebody leave and you sold a house to somebody who lived here, so there's a bloody way out." he said again.

"Robert, Robert Hemlog, or something, that was the name of the guy I sold that house to, or something like that." Paul said.

"Hemlog, or Hedtolg?" Kane asked, wiping sweat from the back of his neck.

Paul clicked his fingers together. "Damn! That's it, Hedtolg, how the hell did you know that?!" He exclaimed.

"Lucky guess, my Doctors name was Hedtolg in the hospital, only his first name was Rod, not Rob". Kane said.

Pauls face went pale. "Jesus, it was Rod, not Rob, that's the name of the guy I sold the house to."

Kane stood there in stunned silence. Both he and Paul lived nowhere near each other and knew nothing of each other, apart from being inexplicably drawn to Finnigan's Point, there was nothing else to connect the two, until now. "Rod Hedtolg is the key, he's the missing link. Somehow he's the reason we are here." Kane said. "I wonder if Gerald or Adam had any links to him?."

"I guess we'll never know." Paul responded. "Let's get back to town and see if the people here remember who Rod Hedtolg is."

The two men climbed back into their cars, turned around and made their way back to town. Kane had been a detective for many years, had solved many cases and was well revered by his friends and peers but this, this was getting more confusing by the minute. He had no idea what anything meant any more. Hedtolg hadn't personally told Kane anything about Finnigan's Point, but the voices and the little girl, that had all happened in the hospital.

Driving back to town, Kane knew one thing, whatever had lured them to Finnigan's Point and whatever this place was, it wasn't normal and it wasn't going to be explainable.

Parking their cars, the two men climbed out. "Where to start?" Paul asked, looking around. Kane had an idea. "I know where to go." he said. Leading the way, he walked towards the grocery store. There were a couple of people shopping in there and Francesca standing behind the till as usual. "Hello stranger," she said, smiling. "You OK?" she asked. Kane wasn't in the mood for chit chat, he wanted to know what was going on and figured the people living in the town must have an idea. "I'm fine thanks, I need to ask you a question though," he replied, not smiling at all. Francesca nodded her head in understanding. "Who is Rod Hedtolg?" he asked her. Francesca said nothing, just stood there looking at him. The two people shopping stopped what they were doing and peered around the ends of the aisles looking at Kane and Paul.

"I know you recognise that name, who is he?" he asked again.

"He's nobody, he lives in town, why?" Francesca responded.

"Because, Francesca, he's the reason Paul, myself and the others have been lured here, he's somehow behind it." Kane said.

"How can he be behind it?" she asked. "How can he be the reason you are here, that makes no sense."

"You're damn right it makes no sense, none of this place makes any sense." Paul said. "Hedtolg told me to come here and a girl in the hospital, Hedtolg's hospital, told Kane to come here."

"So, he would tell people to come here, it's a nice place. Did he tell your other friends to come here as well?" Francesca replied.

"We don't know, they've gone." Paul said, despondently. Francesca raised her eyebrows. "I'm not surprised, you're

133

insane." she said. Paul turned away, swearing under his breath. Kane spoke again, softening his words. "Listen, we're just a bit stressed out, we can't leave this town, we can't get out on the road, it just drives endlessly." he said. Francesca didn't laugh, as he thought she would have done the night before. "Listen, this all sounds very entertaining and surreal, but right now I have customers to serve." she said, looking at the two women who were waiting behind Kane. "Why don't you come over to me for dinner tonight and we can talk about it then, OK?" she said, smiling again now. "Yeah, yeah OK, that would be good, I'll be interested to get your take on things and of course I'll be interested in a home cooked dinner." Kane said, smiling himself. He turned to leave, patting Paul on the back as the two walked towards the exit. Stopping at the door, Kane turned back, in similar fashion to his inspirational hero, Columbo. "Just one thing." he said, raising his finger in the air in the same fashion as Columbo. "You said Hedtolg LIVES here? We thought he moved out?"

"Yes, he still lives here, he comes back from time to time." Francesca replied. "He has a house through the woods, it's the only one on the other side of the woodlands."

One of the women perked up and said something. "Nice house that one, best one in town, only I wouldn't fancy staggering back through those bloody trees after a night on the drink" she said, laughing.

Paul and Kane walked outside. "That's the old house we saw the other day, the one that looked vacant." Paul said. "Yes, it must be and I think we should go and have a proper look at it." Kane said, leading the way. Walking through the woods the two men found the house easily, looking as it had when they had left it previously.

Kane walked up to the small steps and knocked on the door. As expected there was no answer. Walking around the whole of the house, Kane could see that no one was inside.

"I'm going in." Kane said, his hands in his pockets, searching for something. "You can't just walk into someone's house, that's breaking and entering." Paul said, nervously. "In the real world it is, but here, I'm not sure there even is a law and I'm not even sure if everything we see here is real anymore either. I'm going in, whether you come with me or not." he said, pulling a small pen knife out of his pocket. "You going to get in there with that?" Paul asked. "Absolutely, Private Dicks trade tool this is." he answered, jamming the knife into the front door lock. Fiddling around with the knife while Paul looked around nervously, as if the owner may suddenly appear out of nowhere. With a satisfying click the knife turned and the door opened. Kane smiled.

"Coming in?" he asked, pushing the front door wide open.

"No, no, I should wait here in case someone comes." Paul responded.

"Who's coming, Bambi?" Kane asked. You'll be better off behind the closed door. If someone does come, then all they'll find is this empty house."

"What if Hedtolg comes back?" Paul asked. "Good, then I hope he does, we can ask him what the bloody hell is going on here and then he can give us a lift out of town, seeing as he can obviously get out when he wants." Kane replied, walking in. After a couple of seconds of loitering in the doorway, Paul also walked in, closing the door behind him.

The house was well looked after, probably down to the fact it wasn't lived in very often. It appeared normal, nothing there looked odd or out of place. Kane was enjoying being a detective again. He looked everywhere. in drawers, cupboards, everywhere he could think of. Despite appearing large from the outside, inside it was obviously a bungalow, not a house at all. Just one level and all very neat and well placed. Looking in the bedroom, Kane again rifled through the drawers and then made his way to the bathroom. Looking in the cupboards, he could see nothing out of the ordinary. Soap, toothpaste, towels, all the things you would expect to find in a bathroom. Once he had completed a thorough search he sat down in the armchair.

"There's nothing here, so don't make yourself at home," Paul said.

"We need to go." Kane was looking puzzled and not listening to Paul at all. "Strange don't you think?" Kane said, looking up at the ceiling. "Strange? What's strange about this place, its the least strange part of this whole bloody town." Paul responded.

"Hmmmm, maybe, but think about it, not one piece of paperwork here, no magazines, no letters, nothing with a name on, nothing at all." Kane said. "So the guy doesn't hoard shit, where's the mystery in that?" Paul asked. "No, it's like one of those show homes, everything in it's right place, but it doesn't appear as if anyone has every really lived here. It's like a holiday home, you know?" Kane replied. "Well, yeah, it is a holiday home isn't it, the guy doesn't bloody live here." Paul said. "I wish I never bought Hedtolg up, it's probably a bloody coincidence."

"No, it's not a coincidence, there's a link, I just wish we could have established it before Adam and Gerald disappeared." Kane said despondently.

"I hope they are OK, what if they're not and what if we've been drawn here for some awful reason and one by one, we're being picked off?" Paul asked sounding slightly hysterical.

Kane just laughed. "Come on, let's go". he said, leading the way out of the front door.

Once outside the smell of rain hit his nostrils, the air felt heavy with the heat and humidity and he knew they would be hit with a downpour later.

"Listen, I'll go to Francesca's later and see what information I can get on Hedtolg from her. We've made a positive step today." he said. "Oh yes, we've made a positive bloody step, we're still trapped in this town!." Paul responded, sarcastically.

"Yes we are, but we now know of a link between us and a link to Finnigan's Point, we're moving in the right direction."

Paul wasn't so convinced.

"There's only one direction I want to find myself moving in, that's out of this fucking town!" he exclaimed, as the two of them made their way out of the woods. That, Kane could agree with.

Chapter Twenty-Four

Kane stood in the shower, the warm water cascading down his body. He wondered exactly what Francesca would have to say, if anything, how would she react when he told her everything that had happened to him and the others since they got to Finnigan's Point. When he listed the things in his head, it all sounded ridiculous and unbelievable, but even so, it had happened and there was no changing that. With Adam and Gerald gone, Kane was fast running out of people to confirm his story.

Leaving the room, Kane knocked on Paul's door. He answered, looking tired and miserable. "You going to be OK?" Kane asked him.

Paul shook his head yes. "Be fine, could do with a bloody TV in this place though, something to do would be nice."

"We should have taken Hedtolg's," Kane said, laughing.

"You're not wrong, we'll get it tomorrow!" Paul said, smiling.

"Ha, you couldn't wait to get out of there, now you want to go back and burgle him!" Kane said.

"Yeah, fuck him, maybe his fault we're here." Paul said.

"I'm going over to Francesca's now." Kane told him, turning to leave.

"If she says anything interesting, give me a knock on the way back to your room, whatever the time is, I want to know if there's a way we can get out of here."

"I'll be sure to let you know". Kane said, making his way down the stairs.

"You'd better, if you find a way out and leave me here alone to work it out myself, I'm going to haunt you." Paul said, closing his door as Kane disappeared down the stairs.

He made the now familiar walk across town, however instead of going to the bar, made the unfamiliar journey to Francesca's place.

He looked at the flowers she'd planted outside, she obviously took great care of her garden and was clearly proud of it. He knocked on the door and she appeared immediately as if she'd been standing on the other side of the door waiting for him to arrive. She stood there in a long flowing brown dress. Kane was transfixed by her beauty and almost forgot why he was there. "Come in." she said, smiling at him. He walked into her house. Inside it's appearance wasn't too dissimilar to Hedtolg's home, which he'd invaded earlier. The only difference was this home looked lived in. It wasn't untidy, but it had soul. The dimmed lighting helped, as did the smell of the dinner cooking in the kitchen. "Take a seat." she said, pointing towards the sofa and armchair in the centre of the room. "A glass of wine?" she asked, as he made himself comfortable on the sofa.

"Yes please." he replied as he moved the scatter cushions.

"Red or white?" she asked, retreating to the kitchen.

"Either please," he called out, "Whatever you have opened."

A few moments later she returned, holding a glass of red wine, which she set down on the small coffee table at the end of the sofa.

"Dinner will be a few minutes," she said. "I've just got to go and finish a few bits off and then we can go through to the dining area." She returned to the kitchen as Kane realised the dining area was in fact in the living room behind where he currently sat. Francesca had gone to a lot of trouble, the table had been covered in a crisp white tablecloth. On top were place mats, knives and forks and two candles. He admired the effort she had put in for him, especially as she didn't really know him that well. He called out to her. "So what are you cooking then?" He was tempted to go out into the kitchen himself, but having experienced his Mothers temper whenever he got in the way while she was cooking, he decided against it.

"I'm doing a roast dinner, beef?" she called. That for Kane was great news. Since he'd arrived in Finnigan's Point all he'd eaten was pub food, bad pub food at that. He craved some decent nutrition.

"Great, that's lovely." he shouted back to her, while he looked around the room.

A solitary photo sat on top of the television. In it were four people, Francesca was one of them, a man stood next to her and then next to him was a boy and a girl, of about nine and eleven years old. Kane got up from the sofa, holding his wine and made his way over to the photo. Picking it up he looked at it closely. Francesca didn't look much different now, maybe a little younger. While he stared at the photo Francesca walked back into the room.

"You may want to sit at the table now." she said, as Kane put the photo back down on the television.

"Who's with you, in this photo?" he asked, looking round at her. Kane could see a sadness in her eyes and instantly regretted bringing it up. "Sorry, tough question?" he asked.

"No, not at all, no." she replied. She walked over to Kane and picked up the photo. "This was my husband, Brian and these are our kids, Jack and Nicola." she said.

Kane looked into her eyes, which were beginning to well up. "What happened to them?" he asked.

She put down the photograph and went back to the table. "Nothing, I'm just not with them anymore, things happen Terry, you know that." she said.

"You don't see your kids?"

"Not really, sometimes, but not as often as I'd like." she said.

"Sorry I brought it up." he said. "I didn't mean to upset you."

"No, it's OK, you didn't upset me, it's fine, if I didn't want to talk about them I wouldn't have their photo up would I?". she smiled.

Kane sat at the table as Francesca made her way back to the kitchen. She brought a plate through to him and set it down in front on his place mat, before returning with her own plate. He looked at the dinner. Beef, roast potatoes, Yorkshire pudding, stuffing and vegetables, just about his favourite dinner in the world.

He'd had no idea Francesca had a family but had no intention of mentioning it again, it wasn't his business.

"So, what was all that about this morning, with Mr Hedtolg?" she asked him.

"It's nothing really, probably a coincidence. I was in Hospital, Hedtolg was my Doctor. While I was there a little girl told me to come here."

"A little girl? I don't understand, what has that got to do with Hedtolg?" She asked.

"Well, nothing, only I don't think the little girl was real." Kane said.

Francesca started laughing. "See, I knew you would react like this, who wouldn't?" He said.

She stopped laughing and said "OK I apologise, you're obviously very spiritual, I shouldn't make fun, if that's what you think you saw, then you must have." she said.

"Two things" he begun. "Firstly, I'm not spiritual in anyway whatsoever, and secondly, I don't think I saw it, I know I did."

She laughed again. "Well then, that's a contradiction in terms isn't it, if you are not spiritual or don't believe in that side of things, then how the hell can you explain how you saw some apparition, in the form of a child, telling you to come on holiday no less!"

He hadn't thought about it like that and wasn't sure how best to answer. Not believing in God did not mean he hadn't seen ghosts.

"Anyway," he replied, preparing to completely change the subject. "Paul also sold a house, to the same Mr Hedtolg, same guy, explain that?" He said.

"Just a coincidence, so what? it means nothing." she responded. From her mouth it did make sense and everything Kane said was nothing but nonsense.

"Maybe it is, it could be I agree, but whatever the reason, we've both ended up in a town we can't leave." Kane said.

Francesca laughed again, almost choking on a roast potato.

"This I love," she said. "A town you cannot leave, that's genius, how the hell can you not leave? I can't wait to hear this one!"

"OK smart arse, keep laughing. No matter how far we drive, we never get any further away from this town. We can drive as fast as we want or until we run out of petrol and I guarantee we can't get out of the town." he said, indignantly.

Francesca was puzzled and sat with a confused expression.

"Amazing, on the outside you look normal, yet you talk like a crazy man." she goaded him.

"Yeah, laugh it up, I'll show you tomorrow and you'll see, then perhaps you won't find this all so funny as you think it is now. I'm trapped in this town." he said.

"Oh that's nice," she laughed. " You've been trying to escape from me ever since you got here then!"

"Not at all, but it would be nice to leave here when I felt like it." he replied, continuing eating his dinner and for a short while neither of them spoke.

"If you can't get out, where have your friends gone?" Francesca broke the silence.

"I don't know, I wish I did, but they've just vanished into thin air," Kane responded, "and Paul and I are worried we will be next."

"You're worried about nothing, silly, your other friends probably got fed up with this nonsense and went home."

"Yes, I'd like to think that's true, but it's not likely," He was suddenly distracted by the music, playing softly in the background. "What's that?" he asked.

"What's what?" she asked, looking at his plate with a worried expression.

"The music," he said, getting up and going over to the stereo. "Elton John, Honky Chateau, one of my all time favourite albums." he said, picking it up and looking at it.

"Yes, great album, I love Elton John." she said, smiling.

For the remainder of the evening the two of them talked. Francesca discovered a few of Kane's likes and dislikes and he discovered some of hers. As the evening drew to a close, he decided it was either time to make a move on her or go back to the Hotel. Sitting together on the sofa, he thought now was the right time, leaned over towards her. She jumped up as if she'd been stung by a wasp.

"Sorry Terry, but no, I like you, you're a really lovely guy, but I'm not interested in a relationship." she said, still standing.

Kane stood up, he felt awkward and uncomfortable. The soft music, the candlelit dinner, had all that not meant more? He'd assumed it had, but clearly he was wrong. He liked Francesca but decided not to push the point. "That's fair enough," he said. "I've got no problem with that, we're cool." Kane grimaced to himself, "We're cool?!" could I have said anything worse than that?" He guessed not.

"Sorry Terry, I hope I haven't given you the wrong idea." she said, now looking as though she felt equally embarrassed and uncomfortable. "No, of course not, candlelight, low music and a nice meal and a glass of wine, how could I think there was anything between us!" he said sarcastically. "I think it's time you left Terry," Francesca said in response, making her way to the front door and opening it. "Sorry this evening has gone a bit wrong".

"Not at all," Kane responded. "I've had a lovely time, you've been great company."

"I have too," she said, "and great company too, if a little unusual." she laughed. He stepped out onto the front doorstep.

"Thanks for the lovely meal, and don't forget you need to come for a trip in the car, so I can prove I'm not going mad and you are living in a town called Twilight Zone."

"I wouldn't miss that for the World." she replied.

He walked down the path as Francesca closed the door behind him.

Walking back to the hotel, he realised just how quiet it was. Absolutely no sound at all, no animals, not even crickets, complete silence. As he entered the hotel, Gretna spoke to him, which was something she rarely did. "Nice evening Mr Kane?" she asked. He was taken aback, it was the first time she'd asked him anything since the day he checked in. "Yes, fine thanks, I've had a lovely evening." he replied, as he began to climb the stairs.

"Over to young Francesca's for dinner wasn't you?" she asked. Again, he was surprised, how had she known that? Surely Paul hadn't been so bored this evening that he'd actually bothered to strike up a conversation with Gretna Greene.

"Yes, that's right, how did you know that?" he asked, hoping she'd get straight to the point. "Small town Mr Kane, we know everything." she responded.

"Know everything eh? Where's my friends got to then?" he asked.

"I told you, checked out, after that, I have no idea where they go. I'm only interested in the people staying under my own roof." she said. "Like your Husband?, I still haven't met him."

"He's around here somewhere Mr Kane, I'm sure you'll meet him eventually," she said. "Are you sure you had a good evening Mr Kane?"

"Yes, why wouldn't I have?" he asked. "Well, you came back didn't you, if you'd had that good an evening I doubt I would have seen you tonight Mr Kane," she said, smiling at him. "Goodnight Mr Kane."

Kane said nothing, but just continued to climb the stairs, up to his room. As he got to the top, Paul's door opened. "She's a nosy old bat eh?" he said to Kane. "You heard that? She was asking a lot of questions wasn't she, I don't like her much." Kane said. Paul laughed at him. "Ah, she's a cantankerous old dear, you know what old people are like, they are always gossiping. So how did it go tonight, fill me in on the details." he asked.

Kane laughed, "Yeah, and old people gossip don't they?!!" He walked into Paul's room, sat down on one of the chairs. "So, what have you done this evening then?"

"Nothing, been bloody bored actually. I tell you something, I was thinking, if either you or I disappear like the others, then the one left behind is going to go bat shit crazy. Mind you, thinking about it, at least you'll have Francesca to keep you company."

"No, she's not interested in me like that." Kane said.

Paul smiled. "Man, that makes me feel a whole lot better, sorry, but now I know we're both alone. What did she say about our problem?" he asked. "Nothing, she mostly laughed, she thinks we're insane. She's willing to come out in the car with us and show us we're not trapped." Kane replied. "So, she humoured you then, well at least that's something. With any luck, with her living in the town, maybe with her in the car we will actually be able to escape?"..

"We're not getting any luck at the moment, so it would be nice if we could finally get some, God knows, we're owed it." Kane replied.

"What about Hedtolg, did she have much to say about him?" Paul asked.

"No, not really, apparently he already lived here when she got to the town. Most people have a good opinion of him though, seems like everyone likes him. I must say, he did seem like a nice guy when I met him in the Hospital." Kane said. "Yeah, seemed like a nice guy when I sold the house to him as well, until he told me about this bloody place." Paul frowned.

"Well, all we can do is take Francesca along with us and see if that makes any difference to us." Kane said. "Did you tell her about the boat, the shark and the hooded figure?" he asked.

"Do me a favour, I feel mad just talking about those things and I think if I'd mentioned them tonight she wouldn't have agreed on the car experiment." Kane said. "But those things happened Kane, we were both there, we can't deny it." Paul replied.

"I don't disagree, but the simple fact is, these things are only happening to us, they're for us to deal with. I don't think anybody else here is in a position to help us," Kane responded.

"If she comes in the car with us and we do manage to just drive out of here, not only will she think we're definitely nuts, but we'll never be able to talk about this, because no one will ever believe us." Paul said. Kane knew that, but he also knew that if he got out of here, he'd rather not talk about or think about it, ever again. "More importantly than that, Francesca will have to walk back to town for a couple of miles, because I sure as fuck am not driving her back if we do get out." Kane exclaimed.

"I second that," Paul said. After saying goodnight, Kane went back to his room. It was cold. The weather seemed to fluctuate a lot, the day had started off hot and sunny, before progressing to a stormy atmosphere. The rain which had been threatening earlier had failed to materialize and now it felt as though the night had set in for a cold one. Staring out of the window, he looked up at the bright night sky. The moon was full, the sky clear and the bright light of the stars blinked continuously like a billion winking eyes. Whatever Finnigan's Point was, the sky and beyond, was a constant never changing landscape and he took some comfort in that.

Chapter Twenty-Five

Terry and Chris sat, backs against the tree, looking at Harvey's lifeless body. A squirrel came down from the tree and made its way cautiously around the body. Starting at the feet and working its way round to the tops of the legs and then the arms and head, circling the body in a clockwise motion, twice. It wasn't sure what this was, but after a short while it went away, only to return holding some nuts in its mouth, which it proceeded to eat, while sitting on Harvey's chest.

"What are we going to do?" Chris said, staring at Harvey's body.

"I don't know, we need to tell somebody, we can't stay here." Kane replied.

"Yeah and we'll be in big trouble, they will send us to prison or something, I don't want to go to prison Terry". Chris began sobbing.

"It was an accident, we didn't mean it to happen, it was an accident." Terry repeated, looking at Chris.

"What do you want to be when you leave school Terry?" Chris asked him.

"You know I want to be a policeman, it's all I've ever wanted." Terry replied.

"Well you can forget that then can't you, because if you go to prison, you'll never be a policeman."

"It was an accident, we killed our friend, we killed Harvey all for a stupid game." Terry exclaimed, holding his head in his hands.

"We need to sort out what we're going to do, it's getting late and your Mum will wonder where you are Terry."

"So will your Parents Chris," he replied.

Chris laughed. "My Parents? My parents don't give a shit about me."

"Why don't we throw the gun away, make out he was shot from somewhere else, we could say someone was shooting at us?" Terry said.

"We would never get away with that, they'd have our finger prints on the gun for a start." Chris said. "We can wipe the gun and throw it as far as we can, you're a good thrower. It's the only chance we've got of getting away with it, if we use the same story." Terry said, sounding desperate. "OK then, what's the story, how did this happen, someone just shot at us for no reason, we don't know why, they just shot at us?" Chris asked, perplexed.

"Yeah, or we don't even need to say that, all we heard was a bang and then Harvey ...." Terry looked at Harvey and said quietly " and then Harvey ..... died". He looked at the ground, feeling ashamed of himself for wanting to lie his way out of trouble. Chris was right though, his career as a Police Officer would be ended before it began because of this.

Chris thought long and hard, he wanted to go along with the story but like Terry, had a conscience about it. He thought out of the two of them, Terry would get in to more trouble than him because he owned the gun. Chris couldn't see Terry get into that kind of trouble, he knew he wouldn't be able to handle it. The decision had to be his, it was all down to him. A twelve year old boy having to make a life changing decision. He looked over at Harvey's body. Nothing he could do now was going to change the fact that their friend was dead. He could however, change the future for both himself and Terry. Chris knew what he had to do.

"Ok, we'll do it, we'll clean the gun, chuck it and go and get help. We'll do as you said, we'll just say we heard a bang and then Harvey fell to the ground."

"I don't know, are you sure?" Terry said. Chris nodded.

"I'm sure, we need to protect each other, OK?"

"Yeah, OK. The Police will want to know why we left it so long before reporting it, they'll be able to see how long Harv has been lying here." Terry said. "That's easy," Chris replied. " We've been hiding in the woods too scared to come out in case we were shot as well." It seemed feasible to Terry, he thought that as long as they got their stories straight and stuck to it, they could get away with it.

146

Chris wiped the gun with his shirt, cleaning it thoroughly, before holding it wrapped in a dock leaf and throwing it as far as he could. It went some distance and landed quite a way from them.

The two of them walked out of the woods together. They'd entered as three boys and left as two young men, about to tell the biggest lie of their lives. Running down the dirt track that led to the farmers land and then into the farmers field, they heard the angry screams of the farmer again. "Get off my fucking land!" he shouted.

Chris stopped, panting and struggling to breath. "We'll tell him, the farmer." he said through gasps.

Terry was gasping to match him. "He'll kill us." he gasped, struggling to suck in some air.

"He's the closest person, we need to tell him." Chris turned and ran towards the farmer. Terry followed.

The farmer, still yelling, could see the two boys running towards him now, this was a surprise. He stopped shouting and turned to run towards the farm house. His bark was worse than his bite and he really didn't want any trouble from these boys. Naturally Terry and Chris were much faster than the old farmer and caught up to him quickly.

The farmer tripped and landed on his back, just as the two boys caught up with him. Lying on his back, his hands in the air and Terry and Chris standing above him, he spoke.

"Please, please don't hurt me." he said through shaky breath. Neither Chris or Terry were thinking of hurting him and what he was saying didn't really register with them.

"Please, our friend, he's been hurt, we think he may have been shot, we need an ambulance and the police, please, quick." Chris shook the farmers arm.

The farmer immediately jumped up and led the boys back to the house. It was a large old building, every part of it creaked when they went in. He showed the boys into the kitchen, where they sat at a large heavy oak table. The farmer went through to another room and they could hear him talking to someone.

A woman walked into the kitchen, she was a large lady with grey hair and glasses. She had a bright rosy face but her expression was of sadness.

"My husband tells me you boys had had a bit of a shock, would you like a cup of tea while we wait for the police to come?" she asked them. Terry and Chris both nodded. "Good, tea is good for shock you know." she said to them, making her way over to a tin kettle. She filled it with water then placed it onto the cooker top, before sitting at the table with them.

"Your friend, the one you think has been shot, is he OK?" she asked.

Chris started to cry, which led Terry to crying too. Sitting at the big table with this stranger they poured out their hearts, with the well rehearsed story about the bang and Harvey's collapse. They were both genuinely upset, they'd seen there friend shot, but the story they told with the tears was not genuine.

Eventually the police and paramedics arrived and the two boys had to show them the spot in the woods. Once they had got there, one of the policemen took them back to the farmhouse. "We need to call your parents." the Policeman said. "You'll have to call my Mum, Chris is staying with me at the moment." Terry lied. The policeman phoned Terry's Mum and told her to come down to the farmhouse, he said there had been an accident but Chris and Terry were fine. Terry then heard him tell her what they thought had happened and that Harvey was dead. Once he put the phone down he came back into the kitchen. "Your Mum will be here soon son," he said, patting Terry on the head. "While we're waiting I'll take a statement from you both and get it written down."

The two boys proceeded to tell him the same short story they'd told the farmers wife, while the Policeman wrote it down.

Eventually Terry's Mum arrived and took the two boys back to her home. Terry could see she'd been crying as she gave him a big hug, almost crushing his ribs. "I'm so glad you're OK, poor Harvey, his dear Parents, what on Earth are they doing to do?" she said to him.

Throughout all of this, Chris and Terry hadn't paid a great deal of thought to Harvey's parents, it had been self preservation all the way. Harvey was an only child, his Mum couldn't have anymore kids. Now they had no kids and Chris and Terry would forever live with the guilt of the knowledge that they were responsible.

The Police found the gun fairly quickly, a throw to a twelve year old may look like a big throw, but generally it's not as far as it seems. There were no prints on the gun and once it was checked out, it appeared it wasn't registered to anyone. The Police had no reason to disbelieve the boys story and after some more questioning, focused the investigation on the mystery shooter. Of course he didn't exist and six months later the case was officially unsolved. Harvey's parents took the news very badly and demanded answers, but in the end his death was consigned to the annals of history and remained unsolved.

Chris went on to be a Scaffolder, rigging up the scaffolding for the workers. He was twenty one when an accident led to him falling ten storeys. He died instantly. Terry and Chris had remained friends up to that point and now, as far as Terry was aware, it was just him who knew what had really happened on that fateful summers day.

Kane woke up, drenched with sweat. Laying there he felt truly racked with guilt for the first time in years. Looking once again up at the ceiling, he was filled with the guilt ridden thoughts and feelings he'd had the day it happened, as if it was only today Harvey had been killed.

Chapter Twenty-Six

Kane was woken early the following morning by banging on the door again. Climbing out of bed he opened the door, Paul stood there, looking especially relieved as the door swung open.

"Phew, for a minute there I thought you might have gone as well, each morning I wake up filled with dread, I don't want to be the last one left here." Paul said.

"Yeah, good morning to you too," Kane said. "I'll be out in a minute, I'll give you a knock."

"I've packed my bag this time," Paul replied, "You may want to do the same, I have a feeling that Francesca is going to be our ticket out of here." Kane shut the door, laughing. He hoped that Paul was right, he really wanted to get out today, enough was enough.

This morning felt different, he wondered if the culmination of his sequential dream last night had signalled the end of everything else. This morning he felt slightly lifted. For the first time since he'd arrived in Finnigan's Point he didn't bother with a shower, opting instead to throw on some clothes and go straight out. He would have a shower when he got home. As he left the hotel room he was surprised to see Paul already standing there, bag in hand. "Come on, let's go." he said. The two men walked down the stairs, ignored by Gretna Greene who sat at the desk reading a magazine.

"Wait in your car, I'll shoot round the grocery store and get Francesca." Kane said to Paul, who duly obliged and got into his car. It was fairly warm, a nice day.

Kane took a brisk walk round the store and was disappointed upon entering to see Francesca wasn't there, in fact behind the counter was an old lady he'd never seen before.

"Good morning Sir, can I help you?" she asked, as he stood there. "Er, no, you're OK, I was looking for Francesca." he replied.

"Francesca's not here darling," she said. "I haven't seen her for a while."

"She was here yesterday." he said. The old woman thought for a minute and then shook her head. "Not as far as I'm aware she wasn't, like I say, I haven't seen Francesca for a long time, are you sure?" she replied.

"Of course I'm sure, she was right there behind the counter." Kane responded, getting slightly angry.

"No, no, there you are definitely wrong, she doesn't work here, never has done." she responded frowning at him.

Not for the first time in Finnigan's Point, Kane scratched his head in amazement. Turning and walking out of the shop he went straight to Francesca's home and knocked on the door. No response. He knocked again, but still no answer. As he walked away the door opened. There stood, not Francesca, but a man.

"Hello, can I help you?" he asked Kane, looking puzzled.

"Hi, I'm just looking for Francesca." he replied.

The man's brow furrowed. "I'm sorry, I have no idea what you are talking about."

"I was here last night, she cooked me dinner, I was in there." He said, pointing towards the house.

"Unlikely, I was here alone last night and I think I would remember if yourself and some strange woman had dinner in my kitchen, don't you?" he replied, closing the front door.

Kane looked through the window. The interior was completely different to how it had looked the night before, nothing, apart from the outside of the place, with it's well groomed garden, looked the same. "Fuck off"!" the man shouted, banging on the window. Kane jumped back and ran off, back to the car park. Paul sat in the front of his car, asleep. Kane rapped on the window, causing Paul to bang his head on the glass.

"Jesus! What's up?" he said, winding down the window.

"Francesca, she's gone." Kane replied.

"Gone where?" What do you mean, she's gone?" Paul responded.

"She's not in the shop, some woman says she's never worked there and some strange guy is living in her house, it's as if she doesn't exist." he replied, looking despondent.

Paul looked stunned. "Is this some kind of sick joke, because I tell you now, I am not in the mood for it at all."

Kane shook his head. "No joke mate, I'm being deadly serious."

Paul got out of the car and walked past Kane, sitting on the wall.

"You know you were talking about recurring dreams?" Paul said. "Yeah, don't tell me you're having one as well?" he asked.

"Over and over and I think if I talk about it I might be able to leave here. Gerald talked about his accident and I'm willing to bet he was dreaming that incident all the time. After he told us about it we never saw him again. Although Adam never mentioned a dream, he just seems to have vanished." Paul said.

"No, Adam told me he did have dreams, the day he vanished he told me he ran over a little girl and killed her, left her there in the road." Kane said. "Bad, eh?" Paul nodded his head. "Yes, but not as bad as mine, not as bad as my demons." Paul stared down at the ground.

Paul's Nightmare

It was a sunny day in New York. Paul walked through Manhattan and across Central Park. He'd lost his job the previous day, been made redundant. He had always been a great estate agent, but the desire to live in New York really had dropped off since 9/11. Eventually his company had no choice but to make job cuts and as one of the longest serving members of the team, he was sacrificed. The age old adage that it's the last one in, first one out, didn't apply anymore. It was much more cost effective to let the long serving members of staff go and keep on the new, lower paid ones.

Paul had yet to tell his wife. She was, to say the least, controlled by her materialism. She thought nothing of spending a wealth of Paul's hard earned cash on things she couldn't possibly need.

Paul had loved Helen when he married her twelve years before, but over the course of time, he had grown to hate and despise her.

He knew she thought nothing of him, he was her literal cash cow and she'd been milking him dry for years. Despite this, he couldn't bring himself to tell her about his redundancy. He felt like a total failure, despite it not being his fault and he knew Helen would do her utmost to make him feel even worse.

Once he knew the coast was clear and Helen would be out of the way, Paul took the short walk back to the apartment he and Helen shared in expensive Manhattan.

The apartment was huge with three bedrooms. They'd never had any kids and Paul had thought a while ago that the best thing to do would be to downsize and move somewhere more affordable, but Helen had been dead set against the idea.

Sitting in his lounge, with TV playing mindless daytime chat, Paul was disturbed by the front door opening. "Shit." he said to himself. Before he could move Helen appeared in front of him.

"I just rang your firm, apparently you're not fucking there anymore!" she screamed at him. Her dark beehive hairdo wobbling from side to side as she shook her head in anger. "I was going to tell you today." Paul said, still sitting in the chair. Helen stood over him. "Well you should have told me yesterday you fucking useless piece of shit". she exclaimed, spitting her words in anger.

"I'm not useless, I was made redundant, it's just one of those things." He said, getting up and making his way past her and into the kitchen.

"Just one of those things!, just one of those things! If you wasn't so fucking useless they wouldn't have been able to get rid of you, you've always been useless." she screamed at him.

Paul could feel rage building up inside him, he wanted to put his hands around her throat and squeeze the life right out of her. She was driving him insane with her vitriolic rants.

"Any normal wife would be supportive, but not you, you fucking horrible bitch." he said, shouting back.

"How can I support a useless fucking wimp like you, you're pathetic," Helen responded.

The previous day Paul had been fixing the work surface and the hammer he'd left there caught his eye. Picking it up in anger, he shouted at her again. "Shut your fucking mouth or I'll wrap this round your head." Helen started laughing. "Ha, you wouldn't have the guts, you're so fucking useless you'd probably miss anyway." she laughed again. She was still laughing as the clawed edge of the hammer struck her directly on the temple and embedded itself into her skull. Her left eye winking as blood streamed down her cheeks, splashing the white tiled floor with deep crimson.

"You're not laughing now are you, fucking bitch". Paul screamed at her, removing the hammer and repeatedly striking her in the face with it until all that was left was a bloody unrecognisable pulp. He stood over Helen's body, grinning maniacally, before going back to the living room and watching the TV, covered in blood. Helen's body remained on the floor for the remainder of the day before Paul came to his senses and realised what he had done. He had flipped, mindlessly pushed to the brink by her nagging, before jumping over the edge feet first.

154

He knew of a few housing projects locally, which were in the middle of being built and thought he'd be able to bury the body in the cement of one of the homes. Getting the body out of the apartment had been the hardest part. The area wasn't exactly quiet, plus he had to get her down three storeys before he was even at the foot of the building. Waiting until the early hours of the morning, he wrapped her in a roll of carpet and lugged her heavy body out of the apartment. Moving her was a struggle, she was literally a dead weight. Getting the carpet shrouded body into the lift and down to the ground floor was easy enough, but getting her through the foyer, where Harold the security guard was, would be difficult.

Sweat poured down Paul's face, his heart racing a mile a minute, the lift reached ground floor with a ping, the doors opened. The foyer looked empty, no one at the reception desk.

Dragging the weighted carpet across the foyer, Paul froze.

"You OK there?" Harold emerged from the toilet. "Mr Ryan, what on earth do you have there?"

Paul thought the game was up, he was about to go away for the rest of his life. "Nothing Harold, just a roll of carpet I'm trying to get rid of." Paul answered, smiling.

"At three in the morning?" Harold asked, scratching his head. "Seems a bit late, wouldn't it be best to do it tomorrow?"

"It would, it would, but then if I do it in the daytime it'll be harder to dump somewhere, without getting seen, know what I mean?" Paul replied, trying to sound convincing. He reached down and grabbed one end of the carpet.

"Heavy, looks like hard work, Mr Ryan, I'll help you." Harold said reaching down to grab the other end of the carpet.

"Thanks, good quality carpet this, but it's got red wine all over it, can't seem to get it out." Paul said, trying to walk the carpet toward the doors. "Seems a shame to throw it out, perhaps me and the wife could make use of it, if you don't intend to keep it Mr Ryan." Harold said. "No, no, its ruined, I'm getting rid of it." Paul said, getting exasperated. "Let's take a look, it may be ruined for you, but my wife and I, we're not that fussy." Harold said, dropping his end of the carpet to the floor, with a thud.

"No, you can't have it, I'm getting rid of it." Paul said, dragging it away towards the door. Harold stood where he was.

155

"OK Mr Ryan, seems like a shame to get rid of it to me though, still, it's your choice I guess." He said, walking back to his desk and sitting down.

Once out of the door, Paul struggled to lift the carpet into his car, but eventually, after a great deal of effort, made it. Driving round to the local building site, he was relieved to see that one of the foundation bases for a new house still had wet cement in it. Dragging the body out of the carpet, he threw it into the cement. He knew those foundations were deep enough to sink a body, he'd witnessed them building houses before on a walk around with the company director. Helen's body slowly began to sink into the cement. Paul smiled. "Good riddance bitch." he said. He'd wrapped her head in carrier bags, to stop the blood, it had worked. Her bag covered head was all that remained, sticking out of the cement like some oddly discarded shopping. Suddenly, she stopped sinking and all that remained was the head, poking out.

"Oh shit, oh shit!" He said to himself. Looking around he could see a broom lying on the floor not far from where he stood. Picking it up he began to prod the head with the end of the broom, until eventually it started to sink again until all of the body was immersed in the cement mix. The cement looked slightly askew and probably not as flat as it was when the builders left it but Paul figured it would be solid enough by the morning for them to do little about it, other than add another layer. The more the better he thought.

Kane was stunned by the story.

"So there you go, that's why I came to England and that's why I keep having these fucking nightmares." Paul said, rubbing his face.

"I made a career out of catching murderers, I didn't once put you down as being one." Kane said.

"I'm not, not in the common sense of the word anyway, I'm not the type of person who goes around killing people. Helen was a one off, after years of pushing me as well, it wasn't pre meditated." Paul explained. "Don't you feel guilty though?" he asked.

Paul sat silently, not wanting to answer the question.

"Every single day Kane, I've struggled to live with it, that's why I threw myself under a train at Stratford Station.

"You said you'd had no near death experience, you threw yourself under a fucking train!" Kane exclaimed.

"It never occurred to me it was significant. The Doctor's told me I'd been knocked up in the air rather than dragged under it, so I survived." he said.

"Jesus, do you have an idea how lucky that is? Kane said shaking his head. "People don't generally walk away from throwing themselves under a train!"

"Yes, I know, I was very lucky I guess, but I threw myself under it because I wanted to die, it wasn't a cry for help I hadn't expected to survive it." He said

"Anyway, you spoke to Hedtolg before that so it doesn't really link does it." Kane said. Paul shook his head, laughing. "I spoke to Hedtolg after that, it was the first job they gave me after I returned to work." Kane was stunned. "I bet the other two had similar stories about Hedtolg," Kane said. "You should have said earlier, this changes everything."

"I know what this is Kane, I've had an epiphany," Paul said. "I understand now."

"What do you mean, you know, what it is, enlighten me." Kane replied, intrigued.

"We're in purgatory my friend, this is it, the place between Heaven and Hell, it's just a question of where we are going." Paul responded, sincerely.

Kane started laughing. "What a pile of bullshit."

"Laugh all you like Kane, Adam's blow to the head, Gerald's car accident, your shooting and my suicide attempt, killed us all. Repent your sins Kane and you can move on." Paul said.

Kane stopped laughing and thought. "I don't believe in God, it's all nonsense." he said.

"Maybe, but I'm willing to bet that by telling the truth, admitting my guilt and repenting my sins, I'll be leaving here sooner or later and moving on to the next plane. You can deny God all you like, but you've already met him." Paul said. "This is genius," Kane responded, laughing again. "Really, I've met him have I?"

"Rod Hedtolg is an anagram of The Lord God, Kane, I worked it out, is that a coincidence, I don't think so. Think about it Kane, nothing here makes sense, it's not of this earth, you need to repent your sins and you can escape this place." Paul said, getting up from the wall. "I'm sorry Kane, but it's the only answer we were drawn here for a reason and this is it." Paul walked away towards the Hotel. "I'm going for a lie down, today's my day to leave."

Kane sat on the wall, refusing to believe anything Paul had just said. "He's finally lost it." He said out loud, as if trying to convince himself.

Chapter Twenty-Seven

The voice whispered, over and over again. "Paul, Paul," it called. Paul sat in bed listening, this, he thought, was his time. Putting his clothes on, he left the Hotel room. It was late, early hours of the morning, but he knocked on Kane's door. Bleary eyed, Kane opened it. "Jesus, it's late, have you come to your senses yet?" Kane asked. Paul smiled. "It's you who needs to come to yours, I'm leaving." Paul said

"Really, best of luck with that, I'll see you in the morning." Kane said, closing the door.

Paul walked down the corridor and then the stairs. Gretna Greene sat at reception, she looked up and smiled at Paul, saying nothing. Once outside the calling grew louder and Paul could distinctly hear his name whispered on the breeze. Seeing a light over by the woods, Paul knew he had to go towards this.

Kane lay in bed, thinking about what Paul had said. climbing out, he walked over to the window, just in time to see Paul walking through the town, towards the woods. He could see the bright glowing white light and wondered if Hedtolg was in the house. Quickly throwing on some clothes he ran down the stairs. "Going somewhere Mr Kane?" Gretna asked, as he approached the exit.

"Just for a walk." he said, opening the door.

He was outside just in time to see Paul entering the woods, as he ran towards him the glowing light went out.

Standing on the edge of the woods, the darkness surrounding him, it became all too apparent to him, he knew he would have to find out where Paul had gone and maybe solve the mystery of where the others had disappeared to as well.

He entered the blackness, hands extended out in front of him to try to protect himself from the branches that almost skewered his face. There was nothing in front of him, no sign of Paul, no sign of anything. Eventually as Kane's eyes adjusted themselves to the darkness he realised where he now was. Standing just out of sight, he could see the lone house, shrouded in darkness, only this time there were people in front of it, two of them. He could see Paul, he was being spoken to by the hooded figure they had seen on the beach. He couldn't hear what was being said, but he could make out Paul was nodding. He then climbed the steps to the house he'd previously been so afraid of going inside and opened the door. A brilliant blinding white light, brighter than anything Kane had ever seen before, erupted from inside the house and engulfed the woods in it's light. Kane watched as Paul walked into the house and into the light, then the door closed behind him. The hooded figure remained in the darkness, standing at the bottom of the stairs. As Kane was about to approach it, the figure pulled off its hood. Before Kane stood Francesca, her hair flowing in the breeze. Kane watched as she climbed the steps and entered the house, closing the door behind her. Kane ran out from his hiding place and up the steps, throwing open the door. The house looked just as it had last time he had paid it a visit. Throwing on the lights, he could see no one at all. Running around, switching on the lights in each room, he found not a single person. No Hedtolg, no Francesca and no Paul. No one there.

Kane left the house and made his way gingerly back through the woods. As he entered the Hotel Gretna looked up from her magazine.

"Don't you ever sleep?" he asked her, approaching the stairs up to his room. "I'll sleep when the Hotel has no visitors." she said. "You're all alone now dear, aren't you?"

"How do you know that, my friend could be coming back." he said, getting agitated. Gretna just shook her head.

"You sleep well Mr Kane." she said, turning back to her magazine.

Chapter Twenty-Eight

The day dawned and Kane looked out of the window. Once again he had been awoken from the dream about Harvey, this time playing out his death over and over again during the night. He had been wrong, the dream wasn't going away. It was a nice day again but he knew he was alone. He'd watched as Paul disappeared the night before, as did the illusive and seemingly non existent Francesca. He was sure he hadn't dreamt it.

Walking across the landing to Paul's room, Kane gave the door a knock. No answer, as expected. He was officially alone now. He wondered how much truth had been in Paul's rant the day before. He had to admit the evidence was beginning to stack up, the only way he could see himself escaping was to tell someone the truth about Harvey, but who, there was no one to talk to now.

Once he was ready he decided to venture out to the woods again and see if he could find anything in daylight he'd missed the night before. Looking through the leaves, he could see nothing of worth. Once again he circled the house. There was no one in there and no evidence that anyone had been there recently, other than himself.

Leaving the woods, Kane decided to go down to the bar have a drink, there was little else to do.

Entering the bar he could see it was empty, except for the barman, who as usual stood at the bar drying glasses with a tea towel. Kane pulled up a chair and sat down. "Alone today Sir?" the barman asked.

Kane nodded. "Yep all by myself I'm afraid. Pint please."

"No problem," the barman replied, beginning to pour his drink. "Your friends moved on have they?" he asked.

Kane nodded again. "Yeah, moved on, not sure where though, but I know I won't be seeing them again." Kane replied, taking a sip from the drink the barman had passed over to him.

"Yeah, that happens a lot, this place is nice for holidaying but eventually everyone's holiday ends doesn't it". The barman said.

"You're absolutely right," he said, offering his hand to shake to the barman. "Terrence Kane, by the way."

The barman shook his hand firmly. "Brian" the barman said, "But you can call me Brian, everyone does." Kane laughed.

"Yeah, everyone calls me Terry." he responded.

"So Terry, you hanging around here much longer?"

He laughed. "I have no idea, the matter is out of my hands now, I think I'll be here as long as it's deemed necessary Brian." He replied.

"Really, I think leaving here is precisely in your hands Terry, no one else's," Brian responded. "Maybe it's time you faced up to the truth, it's time to move on, like your friends have."

"I don't really see what difference any of that makes." Kane said, drinking his beer.

"Because, Terry, like they say, only the truth can set you free, maybe it's time you stopped fighting." Brian responded.

Kane drank some more of his beer. He wanted out now and he could see no harm in trying Paul's method.

"I killed my friend, when I was a kid." he said. "Accidently I mean, it wasn't deliberate, but we covered it up, me and a friend Chris, we lived with it, never telling anyone the truth."

Brian smiled. "That was easier than you thought wasn't it?" He asked.

Kane smiled. "Yeah it was, it's good to tell someone but to be honest with you Brian, I don't see what difference it's going to make. My other friend, Paul, he believed in God and that admitting your wrongs would free him, I don't believe in God Brian, never have done." he continued, drinking his beer again.

"Terry, you don't have to believe in God for God to believe in you." Brian said, smiling. "Maybe, but either way, as nice as this little chat has been Brian, I don't think telling you my past sins is going to get me out of this place, thanks anyway." Kane said as he turned to leave. "And that, Terry, is exactly what your friend

Chris thought, when I spoke to him." Brian said as Kane walked towards the exit.

Kane spun round. "What?"

Brian was gone, there was no one standing there. Kane walked back over to the bar but it was empty. Brian had disappeared.

He walked outside, surprised to see night had fallen. He'd only been in the bar ten minutes, if that, it should still have been day time. Kane looked at his watch, but it had stopped.

Walking back towards the Hotel, he was stopped by a voice whispering on the breeze. "Terry," it appeared to say. He stopped dead in his tracks. "Terry," it spoke again. "Over here Terry, this way."

Kane looked back towards the woods and there, as the night before, was a white glowing light. He didn't want to go though, the voice, the light, the woods, it all frightened him. He ran back to the Hotel, but as he tried to enter, the door was locked. He began banging on the door frantically. Gretna Greene sat at the reception desk, knitting. She looked up, smiled at him through the glass.

"Mrs Greene can you let me in please?" he asked. She continued to smile.

"Not tonight dear, you've outstayed your welcome, you really need to get going now." she replied, still smiling.

"No, please, please, let me in, I don't want to be out here."

Gretna left her chair and made her way over to the doors.

"I'm sorry Mr Kane, but you know what you have to do now, the wheels are in motion. It's been nice having you stay, it really has, but now it's time to go." she said, and with that, shut the blinds on the doors and windows, leaving him alone outside.

The voice called again "Terry, over here, Terry."

Kane wasn't as alone as he felt. Looking at the light, he knew Gretna was right, there was only one thing to do, only one way to solve the mystery of Finnigan's Point.

Kane walked, slowly, his legs feeling as though they had been weighed down by bricks, towards the woods and the calling light.

Eventually he reached the entrance to the woods and could see the light was further inside. Following the glowing beacon, he walked on, until eventually, as had happened to the others, the light went out. Kane was left in total darkness. Looking around, trying to accustom his sight to the darkness, he could see a shape on the ground. Looking closely, his sight gradually getting used to the sudden darkness, he realised what it was. There, lying in the dark, just as it had been that terrible day in the school summer holiday, lay Harvey. As he leaned forward Harvey sat upright, causing Kane to stagger backwards. Turning his head, with half a smile, Harvey looked at him. One eye blinking while the other was just an open bloodied hole.

"Hi Terry, been a long time." he said, smiling.

Kane tried to scream but nothing came out.

"It's OK Terry, I'm not going to hurt you, I'm your friend." Harvey said, standing up.

Kane stood motionless, he wanted to run away but his legs wouldn't move. "It was an accident Harvey," he said. "I'm sorry."

Harvey nodded his head. "I know you are Terry, really, don't worry about it anymore. I was a little upset you didn't tell the truth, mainly for my Mum and Dad, but that's old news now." Harvey said, holding out his hand to Kane. "Come with me Terry, it's time to go."

Kane took Harvey by the hand. "You're taking me to the house, aren't you?"

"Of course Terry, you've known that all along." Harvey said, leading him into the clearing where the house was situated.

"Thank you for finally freeing me Terry, I've been trapped, waiting for you to admit what happened, I've had to wait, but I can go home now." he said, climbing the steps to the house. The door opened and Harvey smiled at Kane, before disappearing through it. As the door closed Kane could see the hooded figure standing there, Francesca. She pulled down her hood.

"Hello Terrence," she said. "Do you believe in God now?" she asked him.

Kane stood still, looking at her. "Why, where's the evidence of God?" he asked.

"I am the evidence of God, Terrence. I am, and always have been, your guardian Angel. Whether you believe or not, is irrelevant, I've always been there watching you. It was me, in child form, who spoke to you in the Hospital." she said.

"Nonsense," he replied. "It can't have been."

She smiled. "Come with me Terrence, there's no need to fight your beliefs anymore, all will become clear as you walk through the door." she smiled.

"What if I choose not to come through the door Francesca, then what?" he asked.

"Then you stay here for all eternity Terry, never able to leave. This is your one and only chance to move on to the next level." she said.

"What is the next level, Heaven or Hell?"

"That is not my decision, I have no idea what your next level will be, only your maker can decide. You have to go through the door Terrence and face your destiny."

"What about you, what happens to you?" he asked.

"Me? I stay here, I'll always stay here, I'll always be here, until He decides otherwise." she replied.

"Until who decides?" he asked, edging forward.

"You need to go now Terrence, your time is running out." she said, holding out her hand to him again.

Kane was no longer frightened, or nervous, he felt at ease and at peace for the first time in a very long while, he knew he had to walk through the door, he had no choice now.

Walking forward, he passed Francesca and climbed the stairs. He turned to look at her as he approached the door and smiled. "Thank you." He said.

Francesca smiled, "Go home Terrence, you've suffered enough." she replied.

Kane opened the door. The brilliant white light filled the room. His eyes could see nothing more than the blinding white light, but it felt warm, peaceful and inviting. So inviting that he ran into it, the door closing behind him.

Doctor Gordon pounded the patient's chest but there was no use, despite all the efforts he and the team had put in, this guy was not going to make it. "Time of death, 6.40 pm," he said, looking down at the deceased. "Anyone have a name for this guy?" he asked the room, randomly.

One of the Doctors held up a wallet. "Says here his name is Terrence Kane." he replied, looking into it. "I'm sorry Mr Kane," the Doctor said. "We did all we could."

Suddenly the door flew open and a nurse ran in.

"Doctor Gordon, the patient you brought round earlier has had a relapse, he's unconscious again." she said.

"Which one Nurse Fletcher?" he asked. "Wilson, Tony Wilson, Sir." she said, running back out of the room, Doctor Gordon following quickly.

The sterile room quickly emptied, just one Nurse remained and the body of Terrence Kane.

"Yes Sir, can I help you?" Gretna Greene asked the man standing in front of her.

"Erm yes please, I'd like a room for the night." the man replied.

"No problem Sir, we have 4 rooms available at the moment. I'm sure I know you actually, young man, have you been here before?"

"I don't know, maybe, the place does ring a bell." he said.

"Yes, yes, you definitely look familiar," Gretna said, thumbing through her checking in book. "Your name?" she asked.

"Sorry, yes of course, the man said. "It's Tony, Tony Wilson."

The End

Acknowledgements
from Karen Cutler

I would like to thank our wonderful daughter Kelly and our beloved grandchildren Frankie, Ruby, Alfie & Mia for their love and giving us a 'reason'.

Also thanks to supportive friends and family - you know who you are.

Lastly, many thanks to Gwen from PublishNation, for her advice and helping make this dream a reality.

Printed in Great Britain
by Amazon

10209235R00098